CHRISTMAS AT HEMBRY CASTLE

A NOVELLA

MEREDITH ALLARD

A MEDDLING GHOST

*T*he shadows were about again, long along the winding roads, high upon the hills, deep into the valley below, casting a deathly pallor over the tree-lined path leading toward the grand old manor. The castle, known as Hembry in polite society, looked a specter in the night. Accompanying the shadows were the echoes, a sense of a haunting. And why shouldn't Hembry Castle be haunted? The house was ancient enough to have seen three centuries pass and the comings and goings of more souls than it could ever be expected to remember.

Who knew from whence such sounds came? The old floors groaned under whatever weight crossed them. Church-like beams cracked like decrepit bones as they leaned closer toward each other, ever closer. Certainly, the stately home was well tended and much loved, but still it creaked occasionally as the old will do. If you listen closely you might hear footsteps on the curving stairs, whispers in the halls, and flutters of damask curtains caught in open drafts.

The later the time the more menacing the shadows grew.

With the disappearance of the moon behind rain-filled clouds there was little light, leaving long, distorted shapes. Cumbersome trees shed their red, orange, and gold leaves, pointing finger-like branches at the black-looking grass. And still the shadows. Shadows have always provided a good place to hide, especially on a dark autumnal night that threatened wet and cold. Especially for a ghost.

He was a patient ghost, standing back, not wishing to intrude. He hovered near the window and peered into the servants' hall, squinting through the opaque glass that could have used a good scrubbing, hardly a surprise since the servants were busy polishing and buffing upstairs all hours of the day. The ghost glanced about, perhaps a bit nervously, perhaps not. He knew to take care not to be seen. He was not an iridescent spirit, pale and translucent. Had most people in the castle seen him they would have fainted. Has he come back from the dead, they would ask? Has he been stricken by some preternatural magic that gives life to the lifeless? It was the right time of year for it, certainly, as they headed toward All Hallows' Eve. Throughout England were those with their fascinations about magnetisms, perceptionisms, spiritualisms, and other isms. Let the family think what they may. Rather, the ghost decided, let me stay out of their sight so they don't think of me at all. It's better that way.

The ghost was comforted by the sight of the housekeeper at Hembry Castle along with his dearest niece, both on their way upstairs, back to bed, presumably. The ghost glanced at his pocket watch and shook his head, annoyed by the time. What were they doing awake at this hour? The thought of Daphne, his niece, left him hollow inside. How he wished he could be at her wedding! He could not have wished a better husband for her than Edward Ellis—of that he was certain. Edward and Daphne were perfect for one another. He knew it the first time he saw them together at luncheon at Hembry, the way they gazed at each other until they felt other, intrusive eyes drilling them with relentless curiosity, when they turned tomato-red faces to their wine glasses, which couldn't be refilled quickly enough.

The ghost moved away from the castle, not floating, merely walking, certain to stay under cover of darkness. He crossed the grounds at a quick pace and found himself on the outskirts near the decorative mock castles and the Greek temple façades. He stopped at the tree-lined avenue, contemplating his childhood home. He exhaled with pride at the dignity of the place, the sand-colored limestone that rose majestically heavenward, as though its very presence had been ordained by a Higher Force. The winding river crackled as it jumped the stones, the water running faster from the constant rains they had been receiving. He turned to leave, the ghost. He meant to be on his way. Though he was still well hidden, the morning sun would break soon and his cloak of invisibility would vanish.

And yet he could not leave. He walked toward the castle once again, close enough to see through the library window. The ghost sighed. He had been cursed by his birth, landed into an earldom he was not suited to. He wanted to travel. He wanted to do what he wanted to do when he wanted to do it. Suddenly, the ghost saw his younger brother, Frederick, looking rather ghost-like himself as he wandered into the library. Seeing Frederick slumped and downcast, rubbing his hands together for warmth since the fire had died away, the ghost felt guilty. Suddenly, every mistake the ghost had ever made weighed on him. Now he, the ghost, was slumped and downcast, feeling the burden of Hembry Castle that he had thrust on Frederick's shoulders.

Checking upward to see the sky still covered in obscurity,

the ghost crept closer to the old house, sneaking forward like a thief in the night. The library glowed gold from the candles Frederick had lit on the mantelpiece, the light surrounding Frederick like a halo. Finally, with a sigh the ghost felt rather than heard, Frederick sat at the desk, though he stood again just as quickly, pulling his mouth into a flat line. Frederick, Earl of Staton, looked as though he wanted nothing more than to go, perhaps to Sicily, or Luxemborg, or Boston.

Frederick ran his hands through his graying hair. Now nearly seven-and-forty, the Earl of Staton was handsome with his bold features, not unlike the ghost, who would have been 50 years of age on the 12th of August of the Year of Our Lord 1871 had anyone thought to celebrate his last birthday. But the ghost checked himself. He had seen the flowers on his grave in the family plot at the edge of Hembry grounds. He knew they thought of him, spoke of him with great warmth and even a tear or two. He knew they missed him as he missed them.

"I should have given it more thought," the ghost said aloud to the rain now splattering his bowler hat. "I should have considered how my actions would affect my family. Perhaps I've only ever thought of myself when there are so many who think of me." He was embarrassed, the ghost. Ashamed, even.

Peering through windows is never as much fun as one thinks it will be. The ghost wanted to be on the other side of the glass. He wanted to speak soothing words to his brother. The ghost guessed that his brother was thinking of his life before he had been left with the never-ending task of being earl, dreaming of his life in Connecticut with his American wife and American daughter, of a time when he was his own man and free to do his own bidding, which, as earl, he no longer was.

The ghost wanted to examine his brother more clearly but he didn't dare risk being seen under any circumstances. He

4

didn't want his brother or his mother to collapse of a heart attack at the sight of him standing before their eyes, plain as day even in the darkness. These brief glimpses of his beloved family were all that were available to him. This would have to do. Forever, the ghost thought sadly. I cannot be with them. I cannot speak to them. I cannot help them when they need me.

I cannot help them when they need me.

The ghost pushed an inconvenient lock of chestnut hair under his hat. Despite his misgivings, he crept closer still, his eyes focused on his brother's careworn brow.

I cannot help them when they need me.

And then he wondered.

Might I help them? When they need me?

He was nearly in his brother's line of sight now. He watched Frederick, now seated again, his head languishing in his hands. What was causing Frederick such grief? Was there some problem that could be solved, or was it the weight of the mantle of the Earl of Staton? Yet Freddie is such a natural at this, the ghost thought. He handles everything with diligence and ease in a way I never did. It's better that I'm on this side of the glass and he's there. It's better for the castle, the estate, the people who live and work here. Better for everyone.

Except, perhaps, for Frederick.

"How might I help?" the ghost asked the sky. Even from a distance there must be something I can do. But Freddie cannot know that I'm here, that I'm heartily sorry for what I did.

And then the ghost had a thought. He covered his mouth with his hand to stop the laughter from drawing Frederick's attention his way. Of course! He had not done right by his family in life, but he would make up for it now. He would make amends for the havoc caused by his untimely demise. He would help them all.

A glimmer of pink glowed along the bottom of the sky, the

rain easing its dart-like pelts with the coming light. The ghost knew it was time to disappear. But it was all right. He could wait. He would bide his time until he had a plan. It was the least he could do. It would be a challenge since he could only work under the cover of the shadows. After all, ghosts do their best work when no one else can see.

YES, MY LADY

*L*ady Daphne Meriwether awoke in the darkness with a start. Although she had been living in England for more than a year, it was still a shock to open her eyes, prompted by nothing but the uneasiness that she was caught somewhere unexplained, suspended between sleep and dreams, and then, upon awakening, discovering she wasn't dreaming at all—she really was at some strange, unnamed place. For Daphne, that strange, unnamed place was England. More specifically, that place was Hembry Castle, and there she was in her castle bedroom.

She remembered when she first arrived at Hembry Castle. She had heard stories about the stately home from her father, but it was different seeing it for herself. Once inside the manor house she gasped at the hammer beam ceiling, the one installed by the third Earl of Staton to resemble the ceiling at Hampton Court Palace. The walls were dark-paneled wood while marble Roman arches held it all upright. The floors were covered in colorful rugs, and everywhere Daphne looked the long, wide windows let in a panoramic view of the peaks and valleys of the countryside and the winding river crackling and laughing along its way.

Daphne shivered when the deep nips of autumn air chilled her. She pulled her silk dressing gown over her night shift, not that it provided much warmth, but it was all she had at hand. She left her window cracked open despite the cold since her bedroom was easily overheated by the hearth fire. She looked out into the steel-colored haze brought on by the rain, unable to see far into the distance but imagining the leaves falling from their branches, the sogginess of the ground as it soaked up the wet from the cloudbursts. Daphne saw her reflection in glints on the window and caught her breath when she realized how much she looked like her mother.

Of course, she had inherited her mother's gold hair and sapphire eyes, but something in her expression made her think of her much-missed mother. Especially now that Daphne was engaged to the most wonderful man, a writer and editor as her father had been before he became the tenth Earl of Staton. How Daphne wished her mother could have known Edward Ellis. She had no doubt her mother and Edward would have liked each other very much, and it broke Daphne's heart that her mother was no longer here when Daphne could have used her mother's guidance now more than ever. Of course, Daphne loved Edward, but lately he had been... Well, Daphne shook the thought away with a swipe of her hand. She opened the window wider and leaned her head out, admiring the gentle autumn beauty even in the darkness. She hoped for snow but knew it was too soon. Perhaps when it's closer to Christmas, she thought. I would love to see snow at Christmas.

Daphne lit the candle on her nightstand and her bedroom came alive as if the shadows decided to pass the time inside where it was warmer. She marveled at the intricate mural on her cream-colored walls, the painted trees and their thin, outstretched branches, the bird cage, the brown birds, the pink blooms sprouting everywhere. The west wall, the one facing the window, featured a peacock in muted blues. Daphne had asked once who had painted the mural, it was so very beautiful, but like so many things at Hembry Castle it was too old for anyone to remember precisely from where or whom it had come. She closed her eyes, listening to the creaks, the groans, the moans, the whispers, the quick-time patter of the rain. She had learned to find comfort in the cacophony. This is life at Hembry, Daphne thought. The cool of her engagement ring against her warm finger reminded her of its presence. Daphne held it close to her face and smiled.

Edward Ellis. Her fiancé. If staying in England was the price she had to pay to be with the man she loved, then it was a price she would pay, gladly. She thought of his long chocolate-brown hair parted dandily to the right, his wide hazel eyes, his inquisitive glance that took in everything around him at once, his impish grin, his sharp sense of humor. Really, she loved his goodness, his kindness, his hardworking ways, the way he took nothing for granted and stubbornly pursued his goals. And they would be married as soon as they set a date. They should have been married already. They had settled on August, but they decided to postpone after Edward's publishers asked him to write his first book, a Christmas story, with a generous payment to match. After the manuscript was handed in, after he had received his first payment, they would marry. They would set a new date soon, Daphne hoped.

Daphne wandered downstairs, thinking she would like some tea but not wishing to awaken Mrs. Graham at that hour. Candlestick in hand, she tread carefully, not wishing to awaken anyone with her own weight added to the old house's grumbles and sighs. She took care not to trip over the oddly angled stairs, crossing one hall, then another, then down another oddly angled staircase, then across another hall to the green baize door and down another staircase until she found herself in the kitchen. The servants' area was silent, almost eerily so with the absence of the hustle and bustle that kept the place lively during the day and well into the night. Daphne lit the fire in the hearth, turned on the cast-iron gas cooker, poured water into a kettle, set it on the hot plate, and sat before the awakening flames, thinking of nothing in particular when she heard jingling keys.

"Lady Daphne, should you be awake at this hour? And certainly you should have woken Mrs. Graham to fix your tea. That's her job, not yours."

Daphne smiled at Mary Ellis, the housekeeper at Hembry Castle. "I haven't been a grand lady long enough that I've forgotten how to boil a kettle, Mrs. Ellis. When Edward and I move to Staton House, I plan on doing as much as I can myself. I want to live more simply, you know, so that the walls don't have eyes and ears. I don't want to put anyone at Staton House out of work, but I want a more private life for my family. I'm still not used to the servants everywhere. Sometimes I feel them watching me in my sleep."

"You see me watching you in your sleep?"

"Of course not you, Mrs. Ellis. You're family."

"It's good to know I don't haunt my future granddaughter-in-law. Hembry is surrounded enough by ghosts, I think. Besides, his lordship is giving Staton House to you and Edward as a wedding present. You're free to live there however you wish. I happen to know for a fact your grandmother will not be happy to know you're boiling your own kettle, but don't worry. Mr. Ellis and I will never tell." Mrs. Ellis smiled at Daphne with such warmth—a grandmother's smile. "All I wish for you and Edward is to be happy."

The kettle whistled, but before Daphne could stand Mrs.

Ellis poured the boiling water into the porcelain teapot. She spooned in three heady scoops of orange pekoe and let the liquid steep. After Mrs. Ellis poured the tea Daphne gestured to the chair beside her.

"Of course I can't sit with you, my lady."

"Mrs. Ellis, please. I want you to sit and share a cup of tea with me. I want us to talk to each other like any normal family. If I don't have a regular conversation with someone soon I'll burst."

"I'm not sure anyone has a normal family, my lady. We Ellises certainly don't. But you're right. We are going to be family soon." Mrs. Ellis glanced around, perhaps seeking those eyes and ears on the walls, before she sat.

"And maybe you'll start calling me Daphne?"

"Yes, my lady. But after the wedding, and when no one else is near."

"As you wish, Mrs. Ellis."

"You realize, of course, that if I'm to call you Daphne then you must call me Grandmother."

"I'd be proud to call you Grandma." Daphne sipped her tea, listening to the crackling hearth, enjoying the warmth on her skin. "I received a telegram from Edward this afternoon."

"Oh? And what does our prodigal boy have to say for himself? Where has he been?"

"Working, as always, editing the newspaper and writing his essays until he drops from exhaustion. If I don't go to London to see him then I don't see him at all. I'll see him tomorrow, as a matter of fact."

"And it doesn't bother you that if you don't go to London you don't see him?"

"That's Edward, isn't it? Hardworking, squeezing every moment out of his day, afraid of wasting a single minute. Tomorrow while he's busy at the newspaper I'm going to see the seamstress. Edward and I will meet at Staton House in the evening."

"You know he won't change after you're married. No man ever does."

Daphne steeled herself. "Mrs. Ellis?"

"Yes, my lady."

"Has Edward said anything to you?"

"About what?"

"I'm not sure. I know he's working hard as can be. I know he's writing his Christmas book on top of everything else he has to do. But there was something terse in his note. I don't know. Maybe I'm being too sensitive. Maybe I'm imagining it."

Mrs. Ellis gathered their empty cups and placed them in the kitchen sink. "You know our dear Edward's notes. 'I work, I eat, and if I'm lucky I sleep.' What else does he ever have to say?" Mrs. Ellis turned her wide, observant hazel eyes onto Daphne. Edward inherited his keen sense of observation, and his wide hazel eyes, from his grandmother. "Are you worried about something, my lady?"

"I don't have any reason to be. It's just a feeling I've had. I mean, we were supposed to be married in August and it's October now and we still haven't set a date."

"Edward wants to wait until his book is published, my lady, you know that."

"I'm sure you're right, Mrs. Ellis. He just doesn't seem himself lately."

"When you see him tomorrow tell him to forget about that Christmas book. Tell him you insist on setting a wedding date. Let him think about something besides work for a change." Mrs. Ellis glanced at the clock on the hearth. "Now it's time for bed." Daphne followed her future grandmother-in-law through the servants' hall to the staircase. "And Daphne?

Perhaps when you're in London you might talk to the seamstress about your wedding dress?"

"Of course, Grandma."

Daphne nodded at Mary Ellis. The housekeeper's fading yellow hair was piled high on her head, and the plump face was lit as if by her very heart itself, which left Daphne warmer than any hearth fire. Daphne gathered her candle and headed back up the oddly angled stairs for a few more hours of fitful sleep.

YES, MY LORD

*T*hrough the library window you can see across the grounds, across the shaded, park-like land with the benches for sitting in the sunshine when it condescends an appearance, to the imitation Greek statuary, to the farmlands beyond. If you squint through your left eye you can see over the edge of the high hill, which peers precariously into the village of Hembry. From there you have a lovely view of the forest spreading out in all directions. It is, in a word, beautiful.

Frederick, Earl of Staton, knew every beauty Hembry, castle and grounds, had to offer. He spent his boyhood there. As the second son of the Earl of Staton, he had an escape clause written into his birth certificate. His elder brother, Richard, the first of the three sons of the Earl and Countess of Staton, was the one destined to be earl. Frederick, as the second son, had been set for a Soldier or a Vicar. Instead, he carved his own path, becoming first a Writer then an Editor, much to his mother's horror. The Countess of Staton would rather have seen her second son become a gravedigger since, although mere manual labor suitable only to the lowest classes, at least the occupation had some practical merit.

Although it was months since his brother's death, it still took some prodding when someone asked for Lord Staton. It was still a shock when he realized that he, Frederick, was the one being addressed. He was Lord Staton.

In the most private recesses of his heart, Frederick would admit, only to himself, and only on occasion, that he missed his old life. He missed his wife, Diana, who died too young. He missed the rural peace of Connecticut and the contrast of the frenetic pace of New York City. He missed writing. He missed the newspaper business. He missed the rush and bustle of filing stories on time, getting the puzzle of the pages pieced together, rushing it off to the printer at the last minute. Running Hembry, castle and village, was a full time occupation, which left him no time for other pursuits. Hembry was always on his mind.

"A hem!"

Frederick saw the silhouette of Augustus Ellis, the butler, in the long darkness. A man of medium height, thin-framed, hands clasped behind his back, hunch-shouldered and downward looking, Mr. Ellis peered at Frederick over the round wire spectacles perched on his nose.

"Yes, Ellis?"

"Forgive me, my lord. Mr. Feesbury has been searching for you. Have you forgotten the farmers' breakfast this morning?"

"As a matter of fact, I had forgotten, Ellis. Thank you for reminding me. Where might I find Feesbury?"

"He's in your room."

"I'll be right there." Ellis, still in silhouette, remained motionless, his hand on the doorknob, one foot over the threshold. "Yes, Ellis?"

"Forgive me, my lord, but I was wondering if you had

heard. I mean, I heard something of it when I was at the post office, you know, I wondered..."

"For heaven's sake, Ellis. We'll be family when Lady Daphne marries Edward. You are always free to speak your mind to me. You must know that by now."

"Of course, my lord. It's only that I'm wondering if you know why the farmers insisted on seeing you this morning. Naturally, you've heard about the falling prices? There's some grumbling amongst the farmers that lower prices mean less income. Less income for the farmers means less income for the village, and less income for the village means..."

"Less income for the castle itself and everyone who works here. Yes, of course I know, Ellis."

"I didn't mean to imply otherwise, your lordship. But so many on the farms are struggling to get by already."

"Between us, Ellis, I'm not entirely certain what to do about it. Since the American prairies have been opened to commerce our exports are commanding lower prices. But we have our potatoes. They're a hearty crop."

"The Irish might disagree, my lord."

"The Great Famine was nearly 30 years ago. Nothing like that will happen again, surely." Ellis nodded but said nothing. "And don't forget our apples and pears, and certainly our cabbages and peas are enough to keep us afloat. Why, our farmers are ploughing the fields now for the autumn sowing for our winter beans and wheat. We're in the golden age of agriculture, Ellis. This is England, after all. We've become a world power under the reign of Her Majesty, the Queen. Certainly we'll prevail." The butler nodded. "Good heavens. I'm starting to sound like my father. How many times had he spoken in just that way in praise of England and the English?"

"I cannot think of anyone better to model yourself after, my lord."

17

"Nor can I."

Ellis bowed his way out of the library. But the butler's words struck a chord deep in Frederick's brain. Frederick had noticed the frowns lining the farmers' brows the last time he spoke to them, which was just before the harvesting began. He heard the undertone conversations that stopped as soon as he appeared near the fields. Would it be more of the same today? Prying whispers and taut eyes? Frederick didn't know, and he prepared himself for some pointed questions.

The bourgeoning daylight was fully gold now, the vast floor to ceiling shelves and their leather-bound volumes lit as the autumn sun pushed its way in invited or not. Daylight reflected off the mirrors as well as the mirror-like bald head bobbing near the open door.

"My lord." Mr. Feesbury, Frederick's valet, stepped into the room. A nervous, fidgity man, Feesbury bowed in Frederick's general direction. "Really, my lord, you must get dressed so you're ready to meet the farmers. They'll be here any moment for their breakfast."

"And a word," Frederick said.

"That too." Feesbury pulled his watch chain from his waist-coat pocket and pursed his lips at the inconvenient time. "Come along, my lord. We haven't a moment to waste." Feesbury left at such a pace that as soon as Frederick turned around his valet was gone.

ELLIS WAS CORRECT. Though crops were strong, prices had dropped and the farmers were concerned about the profits their bounties would yield. Some already struggled for the rents, which Frederick was happy enough to forget if this turned out to be a difficult season. His father would have done the same, he knew.

They were good people in Hembry. Frederick's father had impressed upon his sons how fortunate they were in that respect. As boys, Frederick and his brothers would sit at their father's knee and listen to stories that sounded fantasy-like, the villains unscrupulous tenants in other areas of the realm who went to ridiculous lengths to avoid paying the rents even when they had the means. But Hembry people were solid Englishmen and Englishwomen who wanted to do the right thing. Of that Frederick was certain.

Frederick stepped outside without his coat and shivered. He sniffed the crisp, clean air tangy with ripened apples wafting from the fields. It was the midst of harvest season, a fortnight past the autumn equinox. Every day men, women, and children went early into the fields to load the carts with apples and pears and cabbages and peas. Further out, the older children cut the brown foliage from the withered potato plants. Since the fertile ground was soaked from the frequent storms, they weren't digging up the spuds yet. Frederick learned that you cannot neglect the tubers too long or else they would rot. Clayton, a youngish man with a brown, shrunken face that looked remarkably like an apple left too long in the sun, said they would dig for the potatoes as soon as they had a dry day, which he predicted for two days from then, after which the tubers would be left to air dry.

For the moment, at least, no one in Hembry, farm or village, was feeling want of anything since the farmers always hired extra hands this time of year to help with the harvesting, the preparing, the shipping, even the selling. As soon as the harvest was collected and carted away, everyone would celebrate the autumn festival together, a feast overflowing with game pies and ale, a thanksgiving for the plentiful bounties of the earth. Frederick wanted this year's celebration to be a good one. From the sounds of it, from Clayton and the others, there may not be much to celebrate in the future if the Americans continued their assault on higher English prices.

Frederick recalled several odd moments with the farmer, Clayton, during the harvest days. Clayton was obsessed with London. He begged Frederick to send him to the city at every opportunity. "London!" Clayton cried. "I must go to London, my lord, and straight away. London!"

"What on earth do you need in London, Clayton?" Frederick demanded. "We have everything we need. Our farms are in good order. I cannot imagine there's anything in London we need concern ourselves with."

"Everything I must concern myself with is in London, my lord! London!"

Frederick sighed. "We'll discuss it after the harvest celebration, Clayton." Frederick could see from the farmer's brow, more wrinkled than usual, that he wasn't happy with Frederick's response. But that was all Frederick would say without knowing more. Besides, Frederick thought, couldn't the man find his own way to London?

Then there was another odd moment with Clayton after he, Frederick, had inquired after Clayton's family. Clayton turned a blank look in Frederick's direction. Finally, after some prompting, as though he had to remind Clayton of his wife and children, Clayton said they were fine and thank you, your lordship, for concerning yourself. There was something in Clayton's manner that made Frederick wonder, but then Clayton left to oversee the potato crop without a single mention of London. Frederick dropped the matter, deciding that Clayton was merely an eccentric man.

"Papa?"

Frederick smiled. "Yes, my dearest Daphne? How may I help you?"

Daphne sat beside her father. "I was about to ask you the same question. You look thoughtful."

"No, my dear. It's nothing. Actually, I've been wondering when you and Edward are going to set a wedding date. Enough about his book already. I thought you might have a Christmas wedding. We need something to celebrate since...well, you know, this will be our first Christmas without your Uncle Richard. I think we'll all want a reason to smile."

"I'm going to see Edward in London today."

"Very good. Now set a date, will you?"

"Shouldn't I consult the powers that be to see when a wedding fits into our social calendar?"

"You set your wedding date for whenever you wish, Daphne. The calendar will accommodate you. I'm the Earl of Staton and I say so."

"As you say, though Grandma might disagree."

"That would be nothing new."

Frederick squinted at Daphne and she squirmed, just as her mother used to when she had something to hide. "Is there something I need to know, Daphne? You can tell me anything, you know that. I will always help you however I can."

"I know that, Papa. And you can tell me anything too."

Father and daughter remained silent. They weren't willing to give up their secrets quite yet. Then Daphne said, "Grandma is looking for you."

"Of course she is."

"Be fair, Papa. She has softened some since Uncle Richard died."

"You're right, Daphne. She has. I'll try to be more patient with her."

Frederick kissed the top of his daughter's gold hair and left to find his mother.

. . .

21

THE COUNTESS OF STATON was discovered in the sitting room, her wide embroidery hoop covering her lap. She was still in black, still mourning her eldest son. After all, it had been less than a year since Richard died. Like Her Majesty the Queen, Lady Staton imagined she would never be out of black again. If Queen Victoria could not get over the loss of her beloved husband, Prince Albert, after nearly a decade, how could the Countess of Staton be expected to get over the loss of her child?

She sat stoically, the Countess, her spine so straight she looked as if she were pulled upward by marionette strings. Only her hands moved, her blue and white embroidery matching the blue and white Georgian vision that was the sitting room, her usual place of residence during the daylight hours. She presided in a throne-like Queen Anne chair, her right foot tapping the blue-green rug in time with her stitches. Frederick shook his head at the portraits of the same black spaniel in various poses. He didn't know which earl's dog it was, but the sight of the animal annoyed him to no end.

"You beckoned, Mamma?"

Lady Staton found the silver ear trumpet attached at the end of a heavy chain around her neck and held the device to her ear. "What did you say?"

"You asked to see me?"

"What do you mean, dear me? Can't a mother ask to see her own son without a complaint?"

"You have no idea."

"What did you say?"

"You have no idea how happy I am to see you every day, Mamma." Frederick smiled. "What did you need?"

"I want to know what Daphne intends to do about that boy."

"Intends to do? About that boy?"

"Really, Frederick. You should listen when your mother speaks." She held her ear trumpet in his direction. "Perhaps you should purchase one. They're rather useful."

"I heard you well enough, Mamma. I don't understand your question. I thought you had come to terms with the fact that Daphne is going to marry Edward. You've been pleasant enough to him when he's come to dine with us."

"Yes, I know, Frederick, but one can never help hoping."

"Hoping for what?"

"Hoping that she might change her mind about that boy."

"Daphne will not change her mind. She intends to marry that boy, who is not a boy at all. He's five-and-twenty, and he's a writer, a talented one at that. They say he's the next Mr. Dickens."

"Are we really in need of another?" Lady Staton dropped her embroidery onto the table. "So she won't come to her senses, then?"

"Daphne has her senses, Mamma. My daughter is the most sensible person I know. She and Edward love each other, and I for one say hurrah. It's my dearest wish to see her happy."

"The butler's grandson makes her happy?"

"Yes, the butler's grandson makes her happy. Now, if you'll excuse me, I have business to tend to." Before waiting to be dismissed, Frederick strode into the hallway and shut the door behind him.

And then he wondered. Should I tell Daphne about the problems the farmers, and therefore all of Hembry, might be facing?

"No," Frederick said aloud, to the peculiar glance of a scurrying maid. "I will not burden her now. This is my problem to deal with, and mine alone."

THE BUTLER'S GRANDSON, OR THE WRITER

The late autumn sunlight streamed through the long window of the study in Staton House, the Earl of Staton's London residence. Edward Ellis, the butler's grandson, also known as the writer, or *that boy* if one were the Countess of Staton, brushed an intrusive lock of chocolate-brown hair from his eyes, attempting to taper down the unruly strands as well as he could with his fingers. He leaned back in the wide-seated chair, staring at the desk pressed against the chestnut bookcase. After staring at the desk lost its charm, he stared at the unused quill in his hand, its tip perfectly sharpened and entirely unused. Then he scanned the titles on the shelves, though he could recite them in order from top to bottom. If he could have mustered the energy he would have plucked a book from its shelf and flipped the pages, searching for something, anything, to inspire him.

Daphne entered the library and he smiled. His golden-haired, sapphire-eyed beauty. His Daphne. He nodded, attempting a stoic exterior, but she was a vision in her peach-toned tea dress with the flowered green trail down the back, the bustle accentuating her finer attributes. Her hair was piled high in plaits and curls. Edward kissed Daphne's hand (they were engaged, after all), cleared his throat, and turned back to the blank page before him. After they were married he could admire her all he liked. Now, he must write.

Daphne peered over his shoulder. "Still nothing?"

Edward sighed. "It will come, don't worry. I've never missed a deadline and I don't intend to start now."

"You still have time. It's not December yet."

"It has to be at the printers soon if we're to have any chance of having it out in time for Christmas. My publishers asked for a Christmas story, after all."

Daphne stepped closer and Edward breathed in her rose-water perfume, grateful for her closeness. "Papa said we should set a wedding date." She watched him, waiting.

Edward wanted to pull her into his arms, say marry me today, now, let's make a run for Gretna Green, to the devil with the banns. But all he said was, "We need to wait until I receive payment for my book, Daphne, and I won't receive my first payment until I hand in my manuscript."

"When do you think you'll have it finished?"

"The writing is harder than I expected it to be. I thought I'd be finished by now and I haven't even started." Edward took Daphne's hand. "But I will finish it, I will receive my payment, and we will be married, Daphne. Of that I can promise you."

Keeping his hold on Daphne's hand, Edward wondered what his problem was. It should be easy enough to write a Christmas story, he thought. Christmas carols. Christmas cele-brations. Certainly Christmas feasts should be enough for anyone to scrape together an entertaining tale. Some prob-lems. Some lessons learned. Why, Mr. Dickens revived a flagging career with the success of his Christmas stories, had he not? Then why am I struggling, Edward wondered?

"I've come to tell you that dinner is ready," Daphne said. "Leave that aside and come eat with me."

Edward set the quill on the untouched paper and followed Daphne to the casual dining room where the family ate when they weren't entertaining. The casual dining room. Edward laughed.

Staton House was certainly well-situated, not far from Buckingham Palace and an easy walk from Hyde Park. Staton House, Number 10 Park Lane, sat stoically in its white row of Georgian style homes. Though most of the house was lightly colored, the casual dining room was dark with mirrors slipped between the mahogany wall panels to reflect the sunlight streaming through the windows on the opposite wall. The long dining table was mahogany, the chairs mahogany, the only things in the room not mahogany, Edward thought, are Daphne and me. He nodded at the young maid serving their meal. The girl had the particular habit of those in service for the Statons—she came and went in the blink of an eye, so quick you hardly knew she was there. When the girl disappeared the table was filled with more food than Edward and Daphne could eat in a week.

"Mrs. Graham sent some of your favorite beef rolls with sage and onion stuffing," Daphne said.

"And syllabub to drink, I see."

Edward breathed in the sherry and nutmeg and nodded. He dug into the beef roll with every enthusiasm that could be mustered over a beef roll and Daphne smiled to see it.

A wrinkle crossed her brow. "Will you be happy living here at Staton House, Edward? I know it's so different from what you're used to. I'm still getting used to it myself."

"My place is with you, Daphne. Staton House is perfect for us here in London. It's not far from the Observer and Fergusonandwately's, that is, if I ever have anything new to show them. Yes, it's grander than I'm used to, but don't forget I grew up at Hembry Castle with my grandparents."

"In some ways it's so different in England," Daphne said. "When we lived in America I never thought about things like where I fit into society. I know people here think I'm living above my place. My father was never supposed to be earl and I was never supposed to be an earl's daughter."

"You know such things aren't important to me. I fell in love with a spirited, intelligent, curious young American woman. Of course, the fact that you can transcribe my shorthand notes was a point in your favor."

"Only one point?"

"One point of many."

Edward remembered the first time he saw Daphne at her grandfather's funeral. He had been struck by her golden-haired, sweet-eyed beauty even if her face was hidden beneath her black mourning veil. At that moment, alone in the casual dining room, he watched her gingerly prod the beef roll with knife and fork in true aristocratic fashion.

"What are you looking at?" Daphne blushed from her cheeks to her nose.

"I'm watching you attend to that beef roll as if you're conducting surgery."

"In America, we'd just pick it up with our fingers. Can you imagine if my grandmother saw me eat with my fingers? She'd die of a conniption."

Edward watched Daphne stab the beef roll with her fork once again. "Go on, I dare you. I dare Lady Daphne Meriwether to pick that beef roll up with her fingers and eat it like the American she is."

"You don't."

"Oh, but I do."

Edward crossed his arms over his chest, leaned back, and waited. Daphne nodded, accepting the challenge. She picked up the beef roll and ate half the pastry in one bite. When she laughed the gravy dribbled down her chin, which she wiped away with her napkin. Edward applauded, to which Daphne curtsied as gracefully as she could from her seated position.

"Do you see what a heathen you're marrying?" she asked.

"You are no heathen, my love. You are everything I hoped you were and more. I still cannot believe that one day soon I shall call you my wife. I am so very grateful for you."

"That's how I feel about you too, Neddie. Which is why I think we should settle our wedding date."

Edward drank his last drop of syllabub and the sugar and sherry warmed him, giving him courage, perhaps? He excused himself and wandered to the window overlooking the garden. The garden at Staton House was not nearly as impressive as the gardens at Hembry Castle, and it all but drooped under the recent heavy rains. Even so, it was far more beautiful than most gardens Edward had seen. He reminded himself that this would be his home soon.

Edward looked at his fiancée as she finished the last of her syllabub. The heat of the sherry and sugar had a beguiling effect and a rose-like blush spread across her cheeks. And he thought, how lucky am I? I'm marrying the woman I love. I'm the youngest newspaper editor in England. My writing career has already risen beyond anything I've dreamed, or it would if I could write that Christmas story. We'll live here at Staton House in London and when we're in the country we'll stay at Hembry Castle where I can be near my grandparents. Edward laughed aloud.

"What is it?"

He was startled to see Daphne standing beside him, so close their arms brushed. "Perhaps I'll become a country house gentleman. Perhaps I'll take up shooting."

"I don't see you as a country house gentleman, Edward Ellis. I see you as a successful editor and writer, and yes, I see you finishing that Christmas story and getting it to your publishers on time."

"You understand me, don't you, Daphne? You understand what drives me?"

"I like to think I do."

Yes, he believed she did understand him. She never argued with him when he said he needed to work. Often, she and her father would arrive at his London flat on Fetter Lane and they would dine together, sharing funny stories about their days. After dinner Edward would retreat to his desk in the side room to write while Frederick read the newspaper. Daphne followed him to his desk and they would chat for a bit, the door open, of course, since they weren't yet married and decorum, you know. Then Daphne would leave him alone to write, bringing him tea and biscuits before he realized he wanted them. Sometimes she brought her needlework and sat silently, her fingers working the embroidery thread through the canvas while he wrote, often late into the night. Edward basked in her silent presence, a balm to his soul.

What is it about this Christmas story that is holding me back, he wondered? What is this blankness in my brain? My whole life I've been bursting with ideas. I've always had too much to write about, not too little. Where is this Christmas story, then? Speak up, won't you? Edward threw his hands up in defeat. Oh, bother with it.

As if reading his mind, Daphne said, "Your publishers need to understand that you're a person, not a printing press. You can't always produce on demand." Edward nodded but said nothing. "Besides, we don't have to wait for you to finish your Christmas book to be married. Papa will help us until you're settled."

"I must be able to support you myself, Daphne. I won't be dependent on your father."

Daphne led Edward back to the study where she had found him. She sat on the brown leather settee and patted the cushion beside her where Edward sat.

"My darling Edward. You always push yourself too hard. But look how far you've come in such a short time. It's only been a year since you started publishing your stories and essays, and look how beloved they are. Give yourself time. Write something else instead."

"At the moment, I'd settle for a grocer's list. Should I write something for the milkman? Do you need cream or yogurt?"

And then Edward knew. In less than a heartbeat he understood his blankness of mind. The clarity blinded him. There it was, a vision of his father, hand outstretched, a beguiling smile, sly eyes on the lookout for any weakness he might take advantage of. Edward felt weak with loathing.

"Are you cold?" Daphne pulled a quilt from the basket and placed it over his lap.

Edward closed his eyes and thought more of his father, though he didn't want to. Holding hands beneath the quilt, with Daphne's head on his shoulder, Edward realized that he hadn't told her anything about his family. She knew his grandparents, of course. They worked at Hembry Castle, after all. Daphne knew his parents, sister, and brother lived in London. She had inquired about them, insisting that it was time their families met. But Edward made excuses. His parents were in Portsmouth, he said, visiting family, even when they weren't. His father was busy at work, he said, even when he wasn't.

Edward knew he would have to broach the subject of his

parents with Daphne. Daphne wanted to set the date, and so did he. But he couldn't live with himself if Daphne felt ashamed of him after she learned the truth. Daphne knew only some of his truth. She knew what he wanted her to know. And the thought frightened him.

THE ELLISES OF BARKING

*E*dward walked at his usual brisk pace along Barking Creek and the town wharf, an inlet of the Thames. The fishing port was not as prosperous as it once had been, but it still flourished, a bit. This area of East London had been little more than a slum before the reign of Her Majesty the Queen but now it had its own railway connecting it to London proper. The area had lost its tenements and gained the London office workers seeking less expensive but still respectable accommodations in the neat rows of terraced cottages. And there, at the north end of North Street, were the red brick semi-detached houses. The Ellises of Barking lived in one such semi-detached house on the north side of the north end of North Street.

He arrived outside his family's home and paused near the door, his hand extended toward the knocker, hanging midair. Normally, he would be happy to be there, eager to see his younger brother and sister, happy enough to see his mother, and not entirely displeased to see his father since, if nothing else, George Ellis had an affable nature. He nearly walked away, Edward, back toward the wharf, back to his flat on Fetter Lane, back to Staton House, even back to Hembry Castle. Anywhere, Edward thought. Anywhere but here.

"Perhaps Daphne and I should emigrate to Canada," he said.

The door answered by way of swinging open and Edward saw his very own sister Kate—since who else's sister would it be?—with her arms open. Even in her green cotton tea dress, with her chocolate brown hair swept back into a simple chignon, Kate Ellis bloomed. Her scalloped green collar matched her eyes, greener than her brother's, and she smiled as if the sight of Edward was the greatest gift ever.

"Edward Augustus Ellis! You never said you were coming. Why are you standing outside? It's going to pour rain on your head any moment now. For heaven's sake, come in!"

Edward shivered, realizing indeed it had grown colder since he arrived. He shook the mist from his overcoat and hung it on the rack while glancing around the small but tidy sitting room. The house struck Edward as rather dark with its mustard colored walls and the green papered wainscoting, the heavy oak furnishings, the shelves covered in bric-a-brac, the red and mustard rugs, and the white damask curtains pulled to one side. It looked, Edward thought, rather ordinary, and he admonished himself immediately for the thought.

"They're not here," Kate said. "Neither is Nathan. They've gone visiting at the Brookings' but they should be home any time now."

Edward looked at his sister, the very spit of him, as so many said. When they were younger they were mistaken for twins. Sometimes, when they were in a mischievous mood, they insisted they were indeed twins, gaining the instant admiration of their friends. He grabbed his sister's hands.

"Kate, I have something important to tell you."

"Is it something good? Heaven knows we need some good

34

news around here."

Edward pulled back. "What has he done now?"

"I'm only interested in your news, which is indeed good news if I can judge by the smile on your face."

"I'm engaged."

"Of course you're engaged. To Christina Chattaway. Have you finally set the date?"

Edward groaned loudly enough to wake the orange striped cat who had been sleeping soundly on the wide arm of the chaise lounge. The cat grumbled with displeasure and disappeared around the corner.

"Oh, dear," Edward said. "I thought I told you. Christina and I are no longer engaged. We ended it some months ago."

Kate eyed her brother through squinted lids. "What did you do?"

"What did I do?"

"Yes, Edward Ellis. What did you do? Did you displease her? Did she grow tired of waiting for you when you were always working? Did you scare her away?"

"Yes. I mean no. I mean I met someone else and I fell in love. I didn't mean to, but I fell in love."

Edward expected Kate to protest. At the very least he expected a fist waved in his direction. Instead, Kate sat in rapt attention, her hands clasped on her lap like a child listening to an adventurous bedtime story wondering whatever would happen next.

"I will always care about Christina," Edward said, "but I didn't love her, not the way I love Daphne. Daphne is special, Kate. She's beautiful and smart and kind and…"

"The truth is, Neddie, I'm not surprised. I never understood what you saw in Christina. She's so quiet you'd hardly remember she was sitting next to you. But didn't her parents complain? They could have sued you. They could have ruined your reputation and career. You could have been the subject for every gossiping old biddy in England!"

"Fortunately, the Chattaways never pressed charges. Daphne's father talked Mr. Chattaway out of making my breach of promise public knowledge."

"How did he do that?"

"I'm sure a bribe had something to do with it."

"You're lucky your future father-in-law was willing to help."

"I'm very lucky, Kate. More than I have any right to be."

Kate leaned close to her brother and grinned. "Her Christian name is Daphne, then? Does Daphne have a family name?"

"Meriwether."

"So how did you meet Miss Daphne Meriwether?"

"Lady Daphne Meriwether."

"*Lady* Daphne Meriwether? Oh, Neddie! Grandmother and Grandfather work for the Meriwethers. You didn't."

"She loves me too, Kate."

"And her family knows?"

"They do. I told you. Her father, the Earl of Staton, intervened so the Chattaways would drop any breach of promise lawsuit."

"What about Grandmother and Grandfather? Do they know you're engaged to the Earl of Staton's daughter?"

"Yes, they know. I begged them not to say a word, Kate. I don't want Pa to know I'm engaged to the daughter of the Earl of Staton."

"But you don't want Ma to know either? Or Nathan? Or me?"

"It's not that I don't want you to know. I was afraid you'd say something in passing to Pa and I can't have him going to my future father-in-law asking for money every time he gets himself into difficulties."

"You're right, Neddie. Even if I am furious with you for keeping it from me." Kate punched her brother in the arm, hard.

Edward flinched, but he laughed. "I apologize. I should have told you. Oh, Kate, you'll like her, I'm certain of it. She's American, did you know?"

"Grandmother told me all about her. Grandmother said she's one of the most beautiful young women she's ever seen."

"But she's more than beautiful, Kate. Do you see? We're well suited. Even Grandfather says so, and you know how he is about these things. You won't tell them will you? Ma and Pa?"

"Of course not. That's your business to tell them. But when are you getting married?"

Edward flung the question aside with a shake of his head. "Think about how many times our grandparents paid Pa's debts when he had to have that gold watch or the most fashionable waistcoat. Every time they told Pa no more money, you're a grown man with a family, you need to mind your own affairs, the creditors would bang on our door at all hours."

Kate nodded. "Do you ever think about the days when Ma would send you with our most prized possessions to the pawn shop?"

"Honestly, Kate, I've done my best to forget those days."

"Pa's problem is he can't hold down any kind of employment. He was released from his last place because some money disappeared only to be found in his overcoat pocket. He's lucky they didn't call the police."

Edward shivered with the thought. "I don't know if you remember, but I was 12 and you were nine and Pa pretended to have a place even after he had been let go. He'd leave in the morning and come back in the evening, but where he had been all day was anyone's guess, especially after his salary stopped coming in." Edward paced, nearly bumping into the tables at either side of the room, trying to vent his frustration. "Oh, he always had some excuse. I didn't want to worry you, he'd say, or it was a mistake and I'll have my place back any day now."

"You never said so," Kate said, "but I know you left school to work to bring in money. I know your teachers said you showed great aptitude."

"Aptitude doesn't put food on the table. Hard work does."

"And Lady Daphne accepts your notion of hard work and the fact that you're working yourself nearly to your death?"

"She understands me."

"And she knows about Pa?"

Edward stopped pacing. "I don't know how to tell her. No one on this earth is happier for my success than she is. No one claps louder when I give a speech in honor of this charity or that memorial fund. But my God, Kate, she's an earl's daughter! How do I explain Pa to her? Her father, Lord Staton, is such a good man, a kind man, a well-centered man who knows what he's about. How can I explain to her what it's like growing up in a home where every knock on the door means the landlord or his bullies are there to collect? How can I explain to her what it's like to hide behind the furniture, silent as a mouse, trying not even to breathe, waiting for the banging to cease and the footsteps to fade away?"

Edward watched the filtered light slip away as the rain beat a ragged rhythm against the window. He pressed his head against the cool glass, slowing his breath, calming himself. It worked for the briefest moment until he felt himself thrust back to his boyhood, back to the pawn shop where he'd sneak close to the door, glancing out from under his slouch cap. When he saw no one he knew, he crept inside and approached the balding, hunchbacked pawn broker, nodding his greetings since they were on a friendly basis by then. Edward would hand over his mother's last pieces of jewelry or a gold pocket watch. Later, Edward would bring coats and jackets and shirts and trousers and shoes and anything else that could be carried out of the Ellis household. The pawn broker would look at the items as though they were junk, not worth his time, but then he'd examine it under his over-large magnifying glass and nod as though conversing with some unseen being who had the final say on the amount to be handed over. Edward had been taught by his mother to haggle at the pawn broker's first price, but Edward rarely did. The only time he haggled was when the hunchbacked man offered a pittance for his mother's filigree ruby ring and Edward, young as he was, knew it was too little. Still, the Ellises had to eat, so he took the money and ran away.

Kate stayed silent, allowing her brother this moment. Finally, she asked, "Won't Lady Daphne understand?"

"I like to think she would. But what if she doesn't? And what about everyone else? What would it mean for my career if people knew about Pa's debts? And what about my Christmas story? Will anyone read a Christmas story from the likes of me?"

"The likes of you?"

"I would be the laughingstock of the literary world, the laughingstock of England if people know who I really am."

"Who you really are, Edward Augustus Ellis, is an intelligent, talented, hardworking man. You are not Pa. You are far more responsible at five-and-twenty than he is in his fifties. People will understand that."

"Will they? Everyone is so quick to judge, so quick to dismiss. And it's not only that I'm worried about Lady Daphne and Lord Staton learning about Pa. I'm more worried about Pa learning about them. We both know what Pa will do when he finds out I'm marrying the Earl of Staton's daughter. He'll flatter Lord Staton, he'll flatter Daphne, he'll flatter Lord Staton's mother, he'll insert himself wherever he can until

Lord Staton becomes nothing more than a money bag for George Ellis. Pa has done it so many times before. How many friends has he lost after they loaned him money he never repaid?"

"What matters is that you're honest with your fiancée, Edward. You need to tell Lady Daphne the truth. You need to tell her about Pa before she hears it from someone else. And you never answered my question. When are you getting married?"

Edward sighed. "We haven't set a date. She wants to set a date and so do I."

"But?"

"I can't afford to support her yet. Besides, I haven't told her about Pa. How can we set a date before I've told her about Pa?"

"Isn't she suspicious?"

"Yes, but she hasn't said so."

"Oh, Neddie. Tell her the truth, tell her now, and set a date for your wedding. Then, after you've set the date, tell Ma and Pa. I'm surprised they haven't read it in the papers."

"We haven't announced our engagement yet."

"At some point it will be announced, and I imagine the wedding will be a society affair. Ma and Pa will find out whether you tell them or not."

"Daphne doesn't want a society wedding so it may not make the newspapers."

"The daughter of the Earl of Staton is marrying the butler's grandson and it won't make the newspapers? That sounds like one of your stories, Neddie."

"Perhaps. Can't I tell Pa and Ma I'm getting married but not whom I'm marrying?"

"You have to invite them to the wedding. They're your parents. And what about Nathan and me? Aren't we invited to your wedding?"

"Of course you are." Edward shuddered. "Can you imagine Pa surrounded by all those aristocrats with his hand out? The mere thought of it makes me want to pull my hair out strand by strand."

"Don't do that, Neddie. You have such a beautiful head of hair." Kate smiled in that compassionate way only a loving sister can. "Don't worry about Pa. Don't worry about anyone else. Think only about the woman you love. If she's as wonderful as you say then she'll understand that not everyone has had a charmed life. Is she some kind of uppity crumpet who thinks life is all song and roses?"

"Of course not. Why, last summer when Daphne discovered her Uncle Jerrold had fathered a child with one of his servants, she insisted on finding the young woman and her child to bring them to Hembry so they could be part of the family."

"All right then. Does she love you so little that finding out about Pa would put her off? Because if that's true, my brother, then you're better off without her. That's all there is to it."

Edward wondered. How much did Daphne love him, really? Was it enough to make up for his childish father? And how would her father feel? Frederick, Earl of Staton, was the finest man Edward knew. Lord Staton must have some sense of Edward's father. After all, Edward's grandparents had worked for Lord Staton's family for more than 40 years. Lord Staton used to say that in some ways Mrs. Ellis was more of a mother to him than his own mother. Still, it was unlikely that either of his grandparents would have mentioned anything like their immature son to the Earl of Staton. More than likely, Lord Staton didn't know about Edward's father, and if Edward had his way, his future father-in-law would never know.

"I don't know if Daphne's unconditional love extends beyond me," Edward said.

"Didn't our grandparents teach you that you should address

her outside the family as Lady Daphne?"

"You are family."

"I'm not their family."

"You're my family. I know Daphne loves me. I've seen it in her eyes. I've felt it in her hands."

"And in her lips?"

"Don't be crass, Kate."

"I'm asking so I can understand."

"I'm sure you are. You should know what Daphne and I had to go through to be together. There were all these mix-ups, and then there was Christina. The fact that we came together must mean that it's our destiny to be together."

"I might have known some of that if you had confided in me, but I understand why you didn't. Neddie, I just realized that your first born son will be the heir to the Earl of Staton. If I remember what Grandmother said, Lady Daphne is an only child?"

"Yes, she is."

"And she can't inherit?" Edward looked at his sister. "So then your eldest son will become the Earl of Staton. You're going to father the, what is it? Seventh earl?"

Edward counted on his fingers. "My son, should Daphne and I be blessed with one, will be the eleventh Earl of Staton."

There. He said it. The thought had been tickling the back of his brain since the day he asked Daphne to marry him, yet somehow he hadn't faced the reality of it until this moment. His son would be the Earl of Staton.

Suddenly, thoughts of the pawn shop, the evictions, hiding behind the furniture, his mother bringing home barely enough to feed the five of them, all of it weighed on his chest as if two well-grown men sat on him, pressing him clean out of air. And then he thought, how can I be the father of one of the grandest men in the land?

"What will you do?"

"I don't know," Edward said.

"You can't spring news of Pa on her after the wedding. She'll never forgive you."

For want of something to do with his hands besides strangling himself with his own cravat, Edward poured himself a cup of tea with the set that had been discretely placed on the table by the young serving girl his family employed. How much had she heard, Edward wondered? From having grandparents at the big house in Hembry, he knew perfectly well how servants' gossip echoed from house to house. Edward gestured to Kate with his cup and she nodded. Edward poured her some tea and they sat together, silent, while sipping the hot liquid.

Finally, Edward said, "You're right, Kate. I have to tell her before the wedding."

They sat silent a while longer. Then Kate asked, "How is your Christmas book coming?"

Edward shrugged.

"That well, I see."

"I honestly don't know what's wrong with me. I'm completely blank, like a giant blotter has wiped away every word I've ever known."

Kate patted her brother's hand. "I think you're making more of Pa's troubles than you need to. I think Lady Daphne Meriwether loves you, and I think she'll understand. And I think her father will too. Beyond that, who cares what others think? People talk. That's what they do. They'll whisper and they'll gesture behind their fans, but that's their problem. You live your life with your bride. Write your Christmas story. Share it with the world and remind everyone of the great talent of Edward Ellis, Author."

"Thank you, Kate. What would I ever do without my dear sister?"

"You'd struggle even more than you do now. So when I do get to meet Lady Daphne?"

"Why don't you come to Hembry Castle for dinner next week? You could meet the whole family."

"Of course, you'll tell Lady Daphne about Pa before I come." When Edward demurred, Kate wagged a finger at him. "If you don't tell her I may have to bring it up at dinner in front of the whole family."

"You wouldn't."

"Wouldn't I?"

"In front of the Countess, the Earl of Staton's mother? Nonsense."

"Then do it, Neddie. Say you'll tell Lady Daphne before I come to Hembry Castle. The longer you dawdle the harder it will be."

Edward sighed. "You win. I'll tell Daphne as soon as I see her again."

"And when might that be?"

"I take the train to Hembry Thursday."

"Very well then. And Ned?"

"Yes, Kate?"

"You realize you're going to have to tell Pa and Ma that you're marrying the daughter of the Earl of Staton. Have Grandfather and Grandmother there. They'll help you say it in the right way. They're good at that."

"Yes, they are. But even our beloved grandparents don't know how to handle our father."

"I know."

Edward grabbed his hat, opened the door, and kissed his sister good-bye.

FATHER OF THE FUTURE EARL OF STATON

*E*dward leaned over the railing at the edge of the Victoria Embankment, peering down into the gray River Thames as it rolled under the bridge. He had stood there so many times, thinking, watching, daydreaming. In fact, he had most of his best thoughts about everything, love, politics, the world at large, standing in that very spot, watching the boats bob and sway, admiring the people stroll or rush. Funny, Edward thought, how the river seemed to change according to the light in the sky. On sunny days the water looked, if not blue, then brighter than the sludge brown it appeared on darker days. Today, with the November sky creeping earlier toward darkness, the river looked decidedly muted, as though waiting for the storm threatened by the ominous clouds.

Edward knew he should get to the offices of the Observer but he was mesmerized by the scenes surrounding him. Life continued no matter the problems of others, he realized. And perhaps his problems weren't so very bad. True, he still hadn't told Daphne about his father. Kate had been to Hembry Castle twice, both times threatening him with silent glares, and both times he had talked his sister out of mentioning their father. Again, Edward promised himself. Next time I'm at Hembry Castle I'll tell her. Daphne has a good head on her shoulders and compassion in her heart. She won't be put off by Pa's misfortunes, even if they are self-created. Next time, Edward promised himself. Next time.

And then the unwanted thought came upon him again: his son would be the future Earl of Staton. An Earl of Staton with a grandfather skipping through the world as if it were his oyster and the pearls were owed to him by his very existence. He could hear his grandmother saying, as she had so many times, "It doesn't pay to worry about something that hasn't happened, Neddie. It may never happen." And she would be right. His father might settle down and learn how to manage money. Edward laughed aloud, prompting a peculiar glare from a well-dressed man in a particularly high top hat. Edward nodded solemnly in the man's direction, then continued toward Fleet Street and Hough Square to the offices of the Daily Observer.

Edward felt better at the Observer since there was work to focus on. He talked to this journalist about his story, to the other journalist about a quick trip to cover the by-election in Lincolnshire. That story needed editing and these pages needed final approval. After he said yes, no, yes, maybe, yes, absolutely never in my lifetime in response to the barrage of questions, he closed his door and breathed. He loved the energy that came with editing the newspaper. Circulation had gone up since he had taken charge. Then he remembered his afternoon appointment and cringed. Usually, he looked forward to visiting his publishers, but not today. He dragged himself away with the air of a man off to the executioner's. He may well get the ax that day, he knew. He had nothing, not one word, to show anyone.

Outside he paced quickly as if he were in a race against the cold. He rubbed his gloveless hands together for warmth, though it did little good. Crisp air filled his lungs and settled him some. Before he knew it he arrived at the offices of Fergunsonandwately. He opened the door with the jingling bell, sending a snapping chill into the room. Edward shivered as he waited under the distrustful eye of an amanuensis. The tick-tock of a pendulum clock snapped in rhythm with Edward's heartbeat, and when the hour chimed he jumped from his chair and dropped his hat to the floor.

Finally, the Wately side of Fergusonandwately stood in state before him. Edward rose to announce that he had not yet finished his Christmas story. He struggled to remain stone-faced while contemplating the sour countenance of Mr. Wately. Mr. Wately tapped a bony finger to his heavily bearded chin, then the top of his arm, then his temple. Then Mr. Wately said, in his most halting air, "And when, sir, do you think you might complete this Christmas story we asked for in May?"

"Soon," Edward said. "Very soon indeed, Mr. Wately."

"If we rush the printer we can give you additional time, but only some. How much time might you need, sir?"

There was something in the tone of Mr. Wately's "sir" that made Edward think his publisher meant quite the opposite.

"Just a bit, Mr. Wately. I'm nearly there."

Mr. Wately lowered his chin in a curt nod. The publisher opened the door and stood at attention, a soldier at arms, making it clear that Edward was expected to return to his desk immediately, chaining himself to his chair if need be in order to finish that Christmas story.

Edward dutifully did as he was bid. After a quick plough-man's lunch he sat at his desk in his Fetter Lane flat. He prepared his ink, sharpened his quill, and readied his paper. If I start writing, he thought, the story will come. Ideas will form, barely at first, but they'll gain strength and pick up speed, snowballs rolling down a hill, faster and faster until I can hardly keep up. I know it. I've done this so many times. But the blank page mocked him. You think you have something interesting to share, the paper said? You think you have something new to say about Christmas that hasn't been said a thousand times before?

Edward closed this eyes. He reasoned that if he couldn't see the paper it couldn't mock him. He held his quill-filled hand at the ready, prepared to begin his tome of a Christmas tale. Instead of writing he cried out as if in pain. He dropped the quill onto his desk, the ink splattering the blank paper like black spots of the blood he would soon shed when he stabbed himself with the nib, which he was determined to do soon enough.

EDWARD TOOK his time on his walk up the hill that led to Hembry Castle. It was the start of December now, the tree branches bare, the sky a chalky color. There had been no snow but the air felt icy, like pin pricks. He pulled his woolen scarf closer to his nose as he braved the slippery ground that forced him to slow his pace. Even in winter Hembry was beautiful, perhaps more so since everything looked so fresh, so pure. Even now, the servants were busy preparing for the Christmas celebrations. What a holiday it will be, Edward thought, his child-like glee overtaking any attempts at a more manly comportment.

It was nearly noon now, and Edward admired the goldenrod sun as it illuminated every iridescent shade in the wet grass. Normally, he would stop to chat with the farmers, the post master, or the vicar, but he was determined to speak to Daphne. He was going to tell her about his father. He was going to tell her everything. He had seen the hurt in her eyes too many times after she had brought up the topic of setting a wedding date and he had demurred. No more. He would marry his darling Daphne, and soon.

"She's an American," Edward said aloud. "She looks at these things differently. She'll understand. Frederick will understand." Edward sat on a rain-wet bench at the far end of the castle grounds, thinking. A cold-braving crow squawked overhead and Edward watched it soar away. Edward wanted to soar away himself, not without Daphne, of course, but rather with her to somewhere where no one knew his parents. The moon, perhaps. His father wasn't in debt on the moon. So far as he knew.

He shivered as the crisp air poked him, particularly on his wet trousers. He turned toward the old house that promised the warmth of a hot cup of tea, a good fire, and Daphne. But instead of walking the rest of the way he remained stubbornly where he stood. He had to get it straight in his mind. What would he say, exactly? He was going to consider it on the train to Hembry but instead he stared out the window, unthinking, unseeing except for the round raindrops splattering the windows. Now that he was here he still couldn't find the words. Fine writer I am, Edward thought. I can't even say something this simple to the woman I love. It was an odd feeling for Edward, this sudden scarcity of words.

He stepped firmly toward the castle. "You're overthinking this, Ellis. Say it as quick as you like and be done with it, man."

Edward shook the wet from his coat and his top hat, exhaled, and strode toward the castle, shoulders back, head high, a man of determination. Instead of turning toward the main entrance he found his way down the hill to the courtyard that led to the servants' door. Then he stopped as suddenly as he started, so much so that his legs wobbled and he nearly toppled over.

Again the pictures in his mind—his father with his hand outstretched before the Earl of Staton. The pinched faces of those who discovered that his father was in debt across England. Everyone who would sniggle about the fact that the father of the future Earl of Staton's own father was insolvent. Edward was ready to turn around, to walk back through the village, when the door opened.

"Edward?" his grandmother called. "Are you coming in or are you a pillar of salt?"

Edward sighed. He followed his grandmother inside the servants' hall and sat at the long table in the dining area.

"Where is Grandfather?"

"Upstairs seeing to luncheon. The family will be eating shortly. Well?" Mrs. Ellis turned a sharp glance onto her grandson. "Are you going to tell her? You realize that God created the world in less time than it's taking you to speak to your fiancée. I know it will be hard, but it must be done. Lady Daphne is hurting, Edward. Are you deliberately trying to distance yourself from her? Do you want to break it off with her the way you broke it off with Miss Chattaway?"

"Break it off with Daphne? Of course not. I love her."

"Then tell her. This is hard for me to say since your father is my son and I love him no matter what he does, but if you've learned anything from your father let it be how you should never treat your wife and family. Don't become a liar, Neddie, not even a liar by omission."

Mary Ellis beckoned a young maid and told her to bring tea and cakes to the sitting room. The housekeeper stood close to Edward, her grandmother's love softening her round face. "My dearest Neddie, I think you took the greatest hit of all, taking responsibility for your family the way you did. I'm very proud of you, and so is your grandfather. Lady Daphne will be too if you'd only give her a chance. She won't love you any the less."

"Do you really believe that?"

"I'd stake every pound I've ever earned on it." Mrs. Ellis gave Edward a gentle nudge on his shoulder. "She's upstairs in the sitting room last I checked. Lady Staton is out paying calls. Go now and tell her. Come, I'll walk you there myself. I'll even stay if you'd like."

Edward followed his grandmother through the servants' hall and up the stairs. He trailed a step behind as they made their way through the winding hallways. As they rounded the last corner Edward's knees quivered and his throat went dry.

"Good God," Edward said. "This is Hembry Castle. She's the daughter of the Earl of Staton. What have I done?"

"You proposed to the woman you love, who loves you just as much. You're going to be married and you're going to live your life without worry about what your father does. He's a big boy and needs to suffer his own consequences."

"You and Grandfather have bailed him out enough."

"You're right, Neddie, we have, and we're determined not to do it any longer." Mrs. Ellis held a firm hand in her grandson's direction. "And no more from you, either, Edward. You have your own life to live. It's time to leave him be."

Mrs. Ellis peeked around the sitting room door and Edward followed his grandmother's gaze.

Daphne sat near the window, perhaps to catch whatever dim sunlight the December day might bring. She wore a peacock blue dress that brought out the violet in her eyes and the high collar emphasized her slim neck. Her gold hair, pulled up in casual plaits, glinted in the sunlight. She took Edward's breath away. An intent smile played up Daphne's lips as she worked her peach thread through the canvas on her lap. Mrs. Ellis knocked lightly. When Daphne saw Edward she smiled.

"Lady Daphne," said Mrs. Ellis. "As you can see, you have a visitor."

Daphne extended her arms toward Edward. "I didn't know you were coming."

"I wanted to surprise you."

"I'm pleasantly surprised."

"Tea and cakes are coming." Mrs. Ellis eyed her grandson narrowly, as though she read his mind, which she could do, he was certain of it. Edward once asked his grandmother how she knew everything about everyone. Did she has especial powers that allowed her insight into the human heart? No, Mrs. Ellis answered. I merely observe people. You'd be amazed what people communicate without saying a word. Edward squirmed under the weight of his grandmother's stare and turned away.

"Thank you, Mrs. Ellis," Daphne said.

With Mrs. Ellis gone, Edward and Daphne were alone. He wanted to take her into his arms and kiss her lips, so he did. With Daphne close, suddenly things weren't so bad. The obstacles brought about by his father were surmountable. He was going to tell Daphne right now.

He opened his mouth and nothing. Where the bloody devil are my words, Edward demanded? Words are what I do. I create worlds with words. I know the swing and swirl of their power as I move them from inside my mind to my hand, and by extension, my quill. Then I take the force of those words to form them into sentences and shapes. I can make words do my bidding. I can bend them to my will. But not any longer. Not this time. When it was most important to find the right words his brain was blank. He grasped Daphne by the arms as though he meant to meld them together. If we are each a part of the other, he thought, then she cannot leave me when she discovers who I really am.

Daphne kissed his cheek, gently, letting her soft lips linger against his skin for a moment longer than perhaps she should have. "Not yet!" others would shout in a stage whisper. "After you're married!" Daphne leaned into him, her head against his chest. Their breath rose and fell together, and Edward wished they could stay exactly this way forever.

"You've looked sad from the moment you walked into the room." Daphne stroked his cheek, turning his face her way. "You can tell me anything, Edward Ellis. There isn't a single thing you can tell me that would cause me to love you any less."

"How did you know I have something important to tell you?"

"I can see it in your eyes. I know every every smile, every laugh, every grimace, every downward glance that tries to hide what you're really thinking, but you can't hide from me. Those huge hazel eyes betray every thought you're thinking, good and bad. Now I see a sadness behind them I don't understand and I want to help. Remember what my mother used to tell my father—a burden shared is a burden halved."

"How did I get lucky enough to find you?" Edward nearly wept from the relief of it. This is exactly what he had been seeking, an easy opening provided by the thoughtful woman he loved.

"Is it your Christmas story?" Daphne asked. "I can take dictation, or I can transcribe your notes, or anything."

"No. It isn't that. Oh, Daphne. It's far more serious than that."

"Whatever it is we'll figure it out, Edward. We'll figure it out together."

Mrs. Ellis opened the door and directed the maid to set the tray with tea and cakes on the table. Mrs. Ellis saw the serious looks on Edward and Daphne's faces and shooed the maid away. The housekeeper watched as Edward and Daphne perched themselves on the settee, their heads so close they touched, and she closed the door behind her.

Daphne poured the tea. Edward stared at his cup, waiting for the words. They'll come now, surely.

"Tell me, Edward. I'm listening."

"It's a long story."

"We have all the time in the world."

Edward closed his eyes. If he couldn't see her perhaps it wouldn't sting so much. "You see my father is…" He sighed. "My family isn't like yours."

"I know, my darling. Your lovely grandparents work here and I don't know how Hembry Castle would function without them."

"I don't mean my grandparents. My grandparents are fine people and I'm proud to be their grandson. It's my father. He isn't… I'm afraid he'll…" And then Edward realized. There is no way to make this right. He felt as if he were strangling, his heart shattering in his chest. It was better to leave now than to hurt her more later.

"I can't talk about it, Daphne. Not even with you. Especially not with you." He took up his hat. "I must go. I have Observer business to tend to."

Oh, but the pain in his beloved's eyes was nearly enough to drive him mad! He should confess, he should, but what if nothing good came from such a confession and he lost her anyway? So Edward remained silent. It was bad enough he would be subjecting the Meriwethers to gossip since he was the butler's grandson. He would not subject Daphne to more embarrassment, more finger pointing, more whispered words behind fluttering fans when the busybodies discovered the truth about George Ellis. And Edward would not subject Frederick to the shame that must come with knowing that his heir was tainted by an unseemly element in the Ellis bloodline.

No, Edward decided despite the hammer-like pounding in his temple. *It has to be this way. I must protect Daphne from any damage I might do her.*

Without turning back because he knew he couldn't face Daphne's anguish, Edward ran from the castle as fast and as far as he could before his grandmother could stop him.

THE GHOST TAKES HIS TEA

*M*rs. Ellis' heart broke for the young woman across from her in the housekeeper's sitting room. Darkness came on quickly now, the only light emanating from the fading rays of the December sun. As the sun fell so did the gloom.

"He won't respond to my messages," Daphne said. "Papa and I went to call on him in London. No matter how hard we knocked it stayed silent inside. Then a floorboard creaked and we knew he was in there. Why won't he talk to me? What is so terrible that he can't tell his future wife? If I even am his future wife. Is that it? Does he want to call it off?"

Mrs. Ellis shook her head. "I shouldn't get in the middle of this, my lady. This is between you and Edward, but this is what I will tell you. I know for a fact that my grandson loves you above anyone else in this world. The sun rises and sets by you as far as he's concerned."

"Then what is so terrible that he won't talk about it, not even with me?"

"I'm afraid I can't be the one to tell you. If there's anything

I've learned from more than 50 years of marriage it's that you have to be able to talk to each other or the relationship hasn't a chance in the world."

"Then my relationship with Edward hasn't a chance in the world."

Daphne dabbed at her eyes with her handkerchief. Mrs. Ellis poured Daphne a glass of water, which Daphne sipped until she settled some.

"I should just accept that the engagement is off," Daphne said.

"Oh no, Lady Daphne. Don't do that, I beg you. Edward will come to his senses. What he has to tell you isn't so very bad. Other families have had worse to contend with."

"So you do know what's troubling him."

"I do, but as I said, I can't be the one to tell you. He has to open his own mouth. He has to speak to you even when it's hard. Especially when it's hard. I'm going to London to try to talk to him myself. I'll take my half-day and go see him. I'll yell at him through the door if I have to."

"Maybe you'll have better luck seeing him than me."

Daphne's voice cracked. Mrs. Ellis wanted to put her arms around her future granddaughter-in-law, because Lady Daphne Meriwether would be her future granddaughter-in-law if she had anything to say about it. But as she was about to reach over her desk the housekeeper stopped herself. Until Lady Daphne and Edward were married such a gesture wasn't proper. Or was it? Mrs. Ellis certainly didn't know.

Then she had an idea. Why, it was obvious. The answer had been there all along, loitering on the grounds, hiding under the cover of the shadows, listening to the whispers on the breeze.

. . .

ONE COULD SAY with certitude that it isn't every day, or every night for that matter, when a ghost comes to tea. To Mrs. Ellis, such spectral visits had become nothing new. She took it in her stride, as she took most things. As the housekeeper at Hembry Castle she had to put out fires, figuratively and sometimes literally, at least once a day. And now, a ghost arriving in the deep, dark night, illuminated by a single candle in the servants' hall, what was so unusual about that? The rest of the down-stairs was silent since the others had long gone to bed. Even Mr. Ellis had made his solitary way back to their cottage. Suddenly, a faint knock rattled the back door. Mrs. Ellis nodded at the ghost, who glowed in the candlelight as he tipped his hat to her.

Inside her sitting room, Mrs. Ellis handed the ghost his cup of Earl Grey and sat across from him, watching him add a splash of milk, drink it down, then gobble away the flaky scone with marmalade at an alarming rate for a spirit.

"Mrs. Graham makes the best scones, doesn't she, Mrs. Ellis?"

"Indeed she does. Would you like another? And more tea, perhaps?"

The ghost nodded. After he finished his second spot of tea and another bite to eat, he leaned back in his chair with his arms crossed over his chest, a content smile on his lips, saying nothing. They had always had a comfortable silence between them. How funny, Mrs. Ellis thought. His whole life all he ever wanted was to get away. Now that he's free he keeps coming back. But that's always how it happens, isn't it? We think we want something until we get it and realize it wasn't what we thought it was. Suddenly, what we had doesn't seem so bad after all.

"So?" the ghost said.

Mrs. Ellis laughed. "So? When you were a boy you used to

stand right there at my doorway," she gestured toward the hall, "with your So? So? So? To everything I ever said to you. So? You haven't changed."

"If I haven't changed by now, Mrs. Ellis, it's unlikely I ever shall." Mrs. Ellis was certain his intense stare would burrow a hole through her forehead. "So?"

"So." Mrs. Ellis nodded, forming the words in her mind before speaking them. "As it happens, some things are not quite right at Hembry Castle."

"But it's nearly Christmas. Everything is supposed to be right at Christmas."

"I don't think anything will be right at Hembry this Christmas. His lordship is preoccupied with some troubles on the farms. And there's something to do with one of the farmers, a man named Clayton, who is obsessed beyond reason with going to London. His lordship has been putting Clayton off, but he suspects Clayton is up to something. So do I, but neither of us have figured out what that something might be. Then Edward never finished his Christmas story and he's certain he's going to be released by his publishers. He's humiliated at the mere thought of it and he feels like a failure. And now he says he hasn't the income to support Lady Daphne."

"Nonsense. Edward is a gifted writer. If Fergusonandwately are foolish enough to let him go because of one missed story then that's their loss. There are many publishers who will consider themselves fortunate to have Edward Ellis. And Frederick will assist them however they need."

"That's what I've told him, but see if he listens to me. But because of that, and some other reasons, he and Lady Daphne aren't speaking and she's thinking of calling off the engagement." Mrs. Ellis exhaled. "I'm afraid it's going to be a rather melancholy Christmas at Hembry Castle this year."

"Indeed." The ghost snapped his fingers as he realized.

"Wait! Did you say there are problems between Edward and Lady Daphne? How could that be? I've never seen two people better suited to one another."

"It's not what you think. I mean, yes, there are problems but the problems are nothing insurmountable if only my grandson would lift his head out of the sand and see it that way. And poor Lady Daphne can't make heads or tails of it because he won't talk to her."

"About what?" The ghost dropped his cup and saucer onto Mrs. Ellis' desk with a rattle. He leaned toward the housekeeper. "What does your grandson have to confess to my niece? He doesn't have yet another fiancée, does he? How many fiancées does he need?"

"Of course he doesn't have another fiancée."

"You must tell me, Mrs. Ellis. I've been searching for a way to help my family. Perhaps this is it. Perhaps I can make amends for all the trouble I've caused by my untimely demise."

Mrs. Ellis tapped her fingernail against her teacup and a hollow ding echoed in the room. She studied the ghost as she considered. Yes, she thought. She would tell him everything. Perhaps he was in a unique position to help after all.

HOLIDAY PREPARATIONS

*P*reparing for Christmas at Hembry Castle was a months-long affair. In September, Mrs. Graham, in consultation with the Countess of Staton and Lady Daphne, created her festive menus for breakfasts, luncheons, teas, dinners, and other celebrations from the first of December through Twelfth Night. She gathered ingredients in October and cooked and baked in November and December. Mrs. Ellis once asked Mrs. Graham how many pies she baked in a Christmas season, to which Mrs. Graham replied, "Somewhere between one hundred and ten thousand million." Everyone always clamored for pies—mince pies, pork pies, turkey pies, pigeon pies, raised game pies, squab pies, steak and kidney pies, roast chicken pies, beef and potato pies, cheese and onion pies, and more mince pies. Mrs. Graham baked enough for the family and their many guests, enough for the villagers, enough for the farmers, enough for all England it seemed. Pies were all Mrs. Graham knew these days.

Sometimes, when Mrs. Ellis was taking tea in her sitting room, bent over the house accounts, her head popped up at the call of "Pies!" ringing from the kitchen. "Pies! Pies! Pies!" When Mrs. Ellis went to investigate, she saw Mrs. Graham and her maids elbow-deep in pastry, nutmeg, sugar, milk, eggs, suet, beef, apples, currants, raisins, brandy, and lemons. Indeed, mince pies were most popular this time of year. Mrs. Ellis always tip-toed away, leaving them to their "Pies!"

A constant stream of visitors flowed through the ancient halls of Hembry Castle throughout the month of December, and Hembry Castle would not be caught out before its guests. The maids dusted every volume in the library, buffed every droplet of the chandeliers until they gleamed, turned on the gaslights, and set glowing candles on the shelves. The footmen polished the silver and laid bowls of pomegranates, oranges, and spices on every flat surface, the scents of cinnamon and citrus filling the air. His lordship and Lady Daphne busied themselves writing Christmas cards, and Lady Daphne made a decoupage display with the colorful cards they received. Mr. Ellis was only slightly embarrassed by the arrival of a box of Christmas crackers ordered by Lady Daphne, who had been so charmed by the bon-bons and poems inside the tissue paper at her first Christmas at Hembry Castle. The butler set his wire-rimmed spectacles back on his nose, coughed, winked, then finally accepted the box from the impatient delivery boy.

Feathered trees lined the shelves, proudly displaying their cotton stars and glass ornaments. The warm spicy scents of the season were soon overpowered by the fresh greens dragged inside by the gardeners, and suddenly the midwinter wasn't quite so bleak. Holly with its star-shaped leaves and red berries was made into wreaths for doors both inside and out. Mistletoe hung discreetly from the Roman arches, leaving giggling maids and grinning footmen scurrying when foot-steps headed their way. Pine boughs lined the banisters and framed every door. Sometimes, after their guests had gone for the day, after they partook of Mrs. Graham's scrumptious delights, as they sat before a hot fire with a good book and a cup of tea, both Frederick and Daphne found some respite from their worries. What they would not admit, even to themselves, was that Christmas at Hembry Castle in the Year of Our Lord 1871 was all a performance with Lord Staton and Lady Daphne primed for the stage. The grand old house looked festive enough, though neither the earl nor his daughter were much in the holiday spirit. Still, they played the role of Gaiety as if wearing smiling Greek masks. Father and daughter did their duty to every guest expecting a grand celebration.

Frederick and Daphne found still another reprieve when some of the farmers dragged in the tall Christmas tree, freshly chopped from the forest. Frederick meant to speak to Clayton, to say hello, to inquire after the farmer's family, wondering if he had made it to London after all. He had heard rumors, you know, his lordship, and he wanted to be certain all was well. Clayton turned his apple face away, slightly less brown in the winter months, ignoring Lord Staton's gestures toward anything resembling conversation.

After the tree was set upright everyone gasped as the highest point nearly touched the cathedral ceiling. By way of Prince Albert, sadly passed nearly ten years to the day now, Christmas trees had become the fashion in England and no stately home was complete for the holiday season without one. After the mess of needles was cleared away it was time to decorate with strings of sparkling beads, candies, tinsel, paper ornaments, and candles nestled within the branches. Everyone, from the maids to his lordship, laughed aloud at the lovely sight. It was, Mrs. Ellis said to a passing maid, the most beautiful tree anyone had ever seen. Hembry Castle looked, sounded, and smelled like Christmas. Then she thought of

Lady Daphne and her grandson and hid her tears behind her handkerchief.

MRS. ELLIS STOOD outside her husband's pantry watching him through the open door. He was involved with the wine lists, as was his wont this time of day. He would take the list to his lordship every morning at 10 am to decide what should be served that evening and at any upcoming special occasions. Today they would decide what should be served for the remaining holiday festivities. There would be sherries and cordials and ports and clarets. There were too many celebrations to count. There was the family's party, the servants' party, the party for the important local personages, and the party for those with titles whether they were important or not. There was the celebration for the villagers and the farmers. There was still so much to do, but Mrs. Ellis set herself, determined to talk to her husband no matter how uncomfortable the conversation might be. This is what she had been telling Neddie, that you must speak to your life's partner even when the speaking might be difficult, and now she must lead by example. She knocked on the door and Augustus Ellis lifted his head, annoyed until he saw his wife. He gestured her inside.

"Since when do you knock?" Mr. Ellis asked.

Mrs. Ellis felt rather than saw his eyes narrowing above his owl-like spectacles. He waited, his elbows on the blotter on his desk, his hands folded, his chin resting on his hands.

"Mary?" Ellis waited until his wife turned toward him. "Whatever is wrong with you? It's not your health, I hope?"

"Oh no, Augustus. Nothing like that. It's only that, well, it's only that I've decided to tell Neddie."

"Tell Edward what, my dear?"

"About me. About who I am. Really."

Augustus Ellis nodded. "I've wondered why you never told him, or George and David, for that matter. Our own sons have never known. And you're going to tell Edward first? Why now?"

Mrs. Ellis braced herself for the rebuke she was certain was coming.

"Because he should have known all along, just as our own sons should have known. Because he's struggling with telling Lady Daphne about George but that's not all she should know, or his lordship, for that matter. I should have told them all years ago but I didn't and now I'm heartily sorry for it. I feel like I've set a bad example for Edward, telling him to be honest with Lady Daphne when I haven't been honest with him. I'm a hypocrite, Gussie. That's what I am. A hypocrite."

Augustus Ellis walked around his desk and took his wife's hands. "You are no hypocrite, Mary Ellis. You are not comparing like with like. What you have to tell Edward is nothing to be ashamed of, and I never understood why you thought it was. You are who you are, and who you are is my wonderful wife who is a dutiful mother and a devoted grandmother. Why, you practically raised Edward, Kate, and Nathan. Edward was here all the time when George..." Mr. Ellis faltered, as he often did when referring to his eldest son. "Well, you know."

"Do you really think I'm doing the right thing?"

"Indeed I do. If Edward has to tell the truth to Lady Daphne and his lordship, he might as well tell them everything. I happen to think both you and Edward are making mountains out of molehills. I love who you are, Mrs. Augustus Ellis, every bit of you, exactly the way you stand before me now. Every time I look at you I'm reminded of the beautiful flower who captured my heart more than 50 years ago. Only today I'm prouder of you than I ever have been." Mr. Ellis kissed his wife's hand. "You're doing the right thing, Menukhah."

Mrs. Ellis flinched. It was the first time she had heard her true name in years. And then she smiled. "I don't know why I'm so surprised, Gussie. I should have known you'd react this way."

Mrs. Ellis closed the door to her husband's pantry and leaned in for a quick kiss on the cheek before some servant set the house on fire. Again.

A DETERMINED GHOST

*T*he ghost hovered in the shadows cast down from the trees, the buildings, and the follies of Hembry land, a caliginous netherworld that had become his home.

He pressed his fingers to his temples as his head spun with Mrs. Ellis' confidences. He thought of Jacob Marley, rattling his chains in frustration as he sought to help those he would not help in life. That's exactly how he felt, the Ghost of Hembry Castle, as he watched those he loved most in the world suffer. Now he was resolute. Now he would help his family in a most single-minded fashion. He wandered the grounds rattling his imaginary chains.

How might I help them? Now that they need me?

His brother was burdened by the tribulations that come with being master at Hembry. His niece was burdened by her fiancé, a fine young man but not nearly as sure of himself as he wanted others to believe. The ghost pulled his scarf closer to his chin, though it offered little comfort against the stinging air. He wished to be inside the castle with his family in front of a roaring fire. He glanced at the sky, which itself looked a specter with a phantom-like storm forming in the distance, expectant with new snow.

The ghost's mind was crowded with half-formed thoughts and ill-baked ideas. He sat on a bench then stood as quickly, afraid of an indecent part of himself freezing to the wood and needing to leave his trousers behind to escape. Instead, he trod quickly, jogging in an attempt to warm himself. He rubbed his fur-lined gloves together though the hands inside stayed numb. He pulled his scarf higher and his hat lower so the two nearly met, leaving a slit through which to see the moon pointing light onto him as if he were center stage at the Adelphi Theatre in London. And all the time he wondered.

What shall I do? Now that they need me?

Let's begin with Frederick, the ghost thought. What can I do for Frederick?

Frederick had been the ghost's partner in crime throughout their childhood. They were practically joined at the hip, as their nanny used to say. The two rambunctious boys would often get themselves into trouble downstairs. With their boisterous ways, they would smack into things, knock over Mrs. Graham's mixtures, and then get a solid talking to over whatever fun they had found for themselves. The ghost thought about Jerrold, the youngest of the three Meriwether sons. Jerrold was not someone the ghost often concerned himself with, even less so after the fiasco over Jerrold's illegitimate child. The ghost's father did his best for his three sons, but Jerrold was always lurking somewhere else, keeping himself separate from the two older boys. He was an odd duck, Jerrold. But the ghost and Freddie, now, they were a pair. They were alike in so many ways.

As it now happened whenever he thought of Freddie, the ghost was overcome. He tried to find some way to reconcile himself to the reality of how he had left his beloved brother to care for Hembry Castle from floor to ceiling, brick by brick, grounds and barns. Frederick had to care for the farmlands, including every family, every cottage, every animal, every crop, every blade of grass. Frederick had to care about sitting with the Lords in London though nothing could be further from his interests. The ghost thought again of his brother's loneliness, how solitary Frederick must feel. It seems such a privilege, being the Earl of Staton, and in many ways it is. Still, it can be one of the most isolating roles in the world.

The ghost exhaled in frustration. I don't know what to do for Frederick, not quite yet. I'll begin with Daphne instead.

The ghost couldn't do much about Edward's missing Christmas manuscript, and he certainly couldn't force Fergusonandwately to keep the young man on, not in his current incarnation as a specter, anyway. But perhaps, just perhaps, if Edward and Daphne reconciled, if the weight of Edward's worries were lifted from his shoulders, perhaps the young man would find his words again.

"All right," the ghost said, talking himself through the process. "How might I nudge Edward along, gently?"

He couldn't make Edward's father suddenly more responsible, certainly not from the way Mrs. Ellis described him, her own son. Edward simply needs to tell Daphne, then, doesn't he. The ghost nodded, answering himself vigorously. Yet Mrs. Ellis had already told her grandson the very same, and she had told him many times. He understood, the ghost, why the boy was reluctant to speak up. But if Edward Ellis is going to become a member of the Earl of Staton's family then he's going to have to toughen up. They were always under scrutiny, the Meriwethers. That's just the way it was.

One thing the ghost knew, to which Mrs. Ellis conceded, is that a skeleton like George Ellis in the Meriwether closet could indeed become an issue for those who enjoyed their gossip.

Still, the ghost mused, the Meriwethers were already subject to speculation, what with the ghost's untimely death and Frederick's taking over the earldom. Then Daphne became engaged to the grandson of the butler and housekeeper of Hembry Castle. Then really, what was one more topic of conversation by way of the fact that the groom's father was indebted across England? Who amongst the aristocratic classes didn't owe debts, many debts, somewhere? It was Freddie's hard work keeping Hembry out of debt. The ghost stared hard at the midwinter night, seeking guidance and finding a void.

The ghost still had no answers, but at least he had some sense of a direction. Perhaps now, before his brain froze to ice, which it was dangerously close to doing, he could concentrate again on Frederick. He wished again for the warmth inside the castle until he realized the brisk night was pressing his thoughts into shape.

He thought of Diana, Frederick's wife and Daphne's mother. Diana had died some years ago, and the ghost was convinced that Freddie was missing her greatly, perhaps even more so now that he faced the cavernous rooms of Hembry Castle alone. One night, peering into the library, the ghost saw his brother with a photograph in his hands. Frederick leaned against the bookcase near the white stone hearth, surrounded by books and a Christmas tree decorated with glowing candles and shimmering candies. It would have been the perfect holiday scene if Frederick hadn't seemed so pensive. The ghost guessed it was a photograph of Diana.

Daphne is a great solace for Freddie, the ghost knew, but Daphne will be married as soon as Edward straightens himself out. Daphne will become deeply involved in her own life, as it should be. It wasn't Daphne's responsibility to always be there for her father. The ghost guessed, knowing his niece as well as he did, that she worried about her father being lonely. The ghost wanted to sit down with her, share a cup of tea with her, tell her that she needed to move on. To be happy. After all, Frederick was the Earl of Staton. He would have no problem finding a wife when the time was right.

And then the ghost wondered. Was it time for Frederick to consider marrying again? What about that widow he had seen Freddie with at Daphne's ball? Mrs. What? Gibson, wasn't it? The ghost had seen the light in Freddie's eyes when he looked at the young, dark-haired widow. At the time she was in black, mourning her late husband. Her mourning must surely be past by now. While it wasn't quite the same way Freddie had looked at Diana, it was still there, the interest, the curiosity. She was rather beautiful, the young widow. How old was she? Older than Daphne, certainly. And Daphne seemed to like her. Perhaps there was something to it. Perhaps Freddie needed a push in the right direction just as Edward needed a push. Perhaps that was his job, the ghost. To push. But how? There were so many factors to consider.

The ghost exhaled and a cloud of icy smoke drifted in the breeze. I'm not there, but I'm close, very close. There's an answer here, somewhere. Perhaps Christmas at Hembry Castle can be saved after all.

CHRISTMAS EVE AT HEMBRY CASTLE

*D*ownstairs at Hembry Castle was all a bustle as it had been for weeks. Poor Mrs. Graham was dusted from her cap to her boots in thick white flour. The powder ingrained itself in every hair, every line on her face, every flourish on her apron, every crevice on the folds of her work dress. No matter how many times a day she washed, ten minutes later she was once again covered in chalky white. If it wasn't "Pies!" it was "Cakes!" and if it wasn't "Cakes!" it was "Puddings!" and if it wasn't "Puddings!" it was "Pies!"

Everyone with flexible limbs who was not of the family or their guests was put to constant use throughout the day and night of Christmas Eve. This maid was needed to fix this green velvet holiday dress with the white fur collar, adjusting the bustle just so. That footman was needed to carry this gentleman's brown leather hunting bag to the stables. A constant hum of rushed footsteps carrying potato balls and Father Christmas shortbread and ham rolls and chestnut stuffing and roast turkey and "Pies!" of every variety could be heard up and down the stairs. The rhythmic stamping of dancing and skipping around the tree echoed in the kitchen. Footmen carried silver bowls of hot punch, mulled wine, and Madeira eggnog, so many bowls that the servants wondered *how much are they drinking up there?* Quite a lot from the boisterous laughter, the barely restrained shouting, and the off-key carol singing. The servants knew they would have their time to celebrate soon enough, with plenty of food, drink, music, poems, bon-bons, carol singing, and dancing of their own.

Mrs. Ellis smiled while directing traffic. She couldn't help herself. The holidays were her favorite time of year no matter the headache of seeing a hundred things done at once. She looked toward the door of the servants' entrance and remembered the previous Christmas. Last year that door had been left open to the cold and the snow, as it would certainly be again this year. The younger servants loved to slide down the snowy mound behind the courtyard, screaming with eggnog-induced laughter. She remembered the flush of red excitement on Edward's face as he and Lady Daphne spent the day dancing and exchanging presents. Is that the day they fell in love, Mrs. Ellis wondered? She had a feeling it had started before then, but she was certain that was the day they both knew what was happening.

Oh! She would wring her grandson's neck, that stubborn mule of a boy, that is, if she ever saw him again. He wouldn't talk to her, or Lady Daphne, or even the Earl of Staton. But what she would say to him as soon as he showed his face again! And why was that harebrained boy hiding anyway? He was acting like he had to confess to being the Rugeley Poisoner. Yes, he had been let go from Fergusonandwately, but Mrs. Ellis didn't see that as being such a terrible thing. They had taken advantage of her Neddie, she was certain of it, paying him a pittance when his stories were so very popular. Was Edward even still in London? Mrs. Ellis didn't know. She thought of

Lady Daphne upstairs, a smile on her lips, a sadness in her eyes, and wished it were last year again.

UPSTAIRS, Lady Daphne, her father, the Earl of Staton, and her grandmother, the Countess of Staton, were the epitome of good English hosts. While hundreds of guests filed into the castle, bringing brisk, cold air and dropping fresh, slippery snow onto the rugs in the front hall, the family presided over the festivities with a genteel decorum that would be expected of Lord Staton's family. During the daylight hours there was hunting for the gentlemen and any ladies who wished to accompany them. For the ladies and some gentlemen who were not inclined to blood sport, which included Lord Staton and Lady Daphne, there were plenty of games of charades and line dances and carol singing to keep everyone merry on Christmas Eve.

After the sky grew dark and the hunters were home from the hills, Hembry Castle was all alight. The gaslight sconces were turned on bright while tapered candles added warmth to every nook and crevice. The postmaster's wife, Mrs. Ebberts, regaled everyone with lively Christmas carols on the piano, accompanied by her daughter, Miss Ebberts, who did her best to sing along. The mother and daughter duo were the very picture of the holiday season in their red toile dresses with red fur sleeves and small white riding hats, which they insisted on wearing indoors. The fires were kept low since the guests, the rum punch, the singing, and the line dances brought their own heat.

Daphne chatted with Miss Ebberts, wishing to thank the youngish woman for her gracious holiday entertainments. Miss Ebberts was beside herself speaking to Lady Daphne Meriwether. At the fifth "Oh dear! I can't believe I'm talking to you, my lady. I'm all afluttered!" Daphne smiled, thanked Miss Ebberts once again, then excused herself. She walked into the wide central room where guests danced the Queen's Waltz. Two couples put their right hands in, traveled forward, put their left hands in, traveled forward. Daphne watched as they skipped and peeled. Last Christmas she and Edward had danced the day away together. They were so happy. What had happened? Daphne didn't know. At the moment she would settle for a simple conversation with him. She had decided that the engagement was definitely off. She hadn't admitted it yet, not out loud, not to anyone, not even to her father who had always been her most trusted of confidants.

Of course, he had guessed, Papa. He had asked her several times, "When is Edward coming to celebrate Christmas with us?" or "Why haven't you set a wedding date? Are you and Edward having problems between you, Daphne?" And Daphne would insist no, absolutely not, never. Edward and I love each other. Edward and I are getting married. Her father would nod, his eyes small because he understood what she wouldn't say. But since she had not confided in him, he would not intrude. It's better this way, Daphne thought. Papa has enough troubles of his own. He wants to fix everything for everyone, which is one of the many reasons I love him so.

Daphne passed the gilded mirror on the wall in the drawing room where the titled guests gathered to toast each other's health again and again. She caught a glimpse of herself, her hair adorned with green lace ribbons and stacked high on her head, her festive dress made especially for this day, deep green velvet adorned with white rosettes, the back tapering to her bustle and falling in ripples to the top of her white boots. When she had the dress made she thought she and Edward might marry sometime this Christmas season. She had thought so many things.

Yes, her heart was broken, but her heart had been broken before. When her mother died, and then her grandfather, she was shattered every which way, but she mended, and she survived. Although the pain of Edward's loss was physical, as if she were poked by knives, she would survive this too. For now, she must smile. She must smile and chat and watch others enjoy the delicious bites that Mrs. Graham had prepared. As Daphne turned to leave she nodded at the woman who caught her eye, some Lady Whatever dripping in rubies and emeralds, but Daphne escaped before having to speak to anyone.

Free from the prying eyes of the titled whoevers, Daphne headed upstairs for a few moments of peace. She stopped at the sound of a woman singing "Silent Night." This wasn't one of Miss Ebberts' well intentioned attempts, but rather something plaintive and ultimately beautiful. Who was singing? Daphne didn't know. She only knew that the high pitched dulcet tones filled her with deep longing.

Silent night, holy night
All is calm, all is bright
Round yon Virgin, Mother and Child
Holy infant so tender and mild
Sleep in heavenly peace
Sleep in heavenly peace

Daphne dabbed her eyes with the back of her hand. She turned toward the staircase and saw Mr. Ellis supervising the footmen as they delivered platters with food and drink. Daphne steeled herself. The Ellises were Edward's grandparents and they were employed by her father. She would continue to see them all day, every day, until they retired. They were good people, the Ellises. She loved having them around, and certainly Hembry Castle could never function without them. When Mr. Ellis saw her, he nodded, once, but there was much feeling in the gesture. It took every ounce of strength

Daphne had to hold her anguish inside until she escaped into the sanctuary of her bedroom.

IT WASN'T DARK this Christmas Eve, not yet. The sun was only beginning to set and the sky blushed pink and white as the delicate snowflakes fell, leaving soft pillows on the ground. The holiday revelries inside Hembry Castle grew more raucous the later the time grew. Several guests left for other celebrations. For some, the number of festivities they attended were a badge of honor. Others were quite happy to continue the holiday entertainments in the hallowed halls of Hembry Castle.

It was a dangerous hour for ghosts to be about, this in-between time, but he was a ghost on a mission. The snow fell faster, leaving a fresh white blanket weighing down the bare-branched trees, stretching across the grounds, covering the very castle itself in pristine radiance. The ghost, immune to the icy air, numb as he was, lingered near the servants' courtyard, close but not so close. He was near enough to see the younger servants dancing to an out of tune violin playing "Ding Dong, Merrily on High" while others slipped and slid down the snowy embankment. The servants were so caught up in their merrymaking they weren't likely to notice him. He was an unobtrusive ghost, after all. But he couldn't take a chance that he might be seen. He stepped behind the wall of the courtyard and waited.

"So?" he heard from the other side of the wall.

"So?"

"Are you ready?"

"This is the moment I've been waiting for," the ghost said. "I'm ready."

. . .

THE HOURS PASSED. The night grew later and darker and the grounds grew whiter. It would be rude to yawn in front of his guests, so Frederick, Lord Staton, helped himself to some hot water and the last scoop of darjeeling at the side table where guests had been feasting on small dishes of quails eggs, truffle potatoes, fried smelts, roast turkey, and of course Mrs. Graham's delicious pies. He could never get enough of them. He wasn't hungry himself, Frederick, but he enjoyed watching his guests savor every delectable dish. Mrs. Graham had worked so very hard, after all. He sipped his tea, but instead of a burst of energy he felt lethargic until the sight of a fresh snowfall brightened him. He had always loved the snow in winter, and especially he had always loved Christmas at Hembry Castle. Yes, this year was different when last year had been so joyful. But this too shall pass, Frederick thought. Everything, both good and bad, changes with time and we must make the best of it, good and bad. We learn what we need to learn from each experience, good and bad, and we carry on, doing the best we can at every turn.

Frederick stared through the window at the deepening gray haze coming down from the north, which meant the snow was likely to continue until morning. He startled when a loud "Your lordship!" came from behind. He turned to see Mrs. Ellis pressing a silver tray with a letter in his direction.

"Excuse me, my lord. I'm sorry to disturb you."

"You're not disturbing me, Mrs. Ellis. Not at all."

"I'm afraid you were looking rather contemplative."

Soft heels of a genteel country dance echoed into the room.

"I'm not certain one can be contemplative on such a day." Frederick nodded at the silver tray. "Are you the butler here now?"

"Mr. Ellis is busy downstairs so I told him you wouldn't mind if I brought this. It seemed urgent."

She pressed the tray closer to Frederick. He sighed, but he took the letter and the opener, sliced the envelope, and read the contents. He read once, read twice, read a third time just to be certain, then slid the letter back into the envelope and into his breast pocket.

"Who sent this?" he asked.

"I couldn't say, my lord. I was told it was left outside the door, and as you can see the envelope is addressed to you."

Mrs. Ellis waited while he took the letter from his pocket to read once more.

"I'm afraid I must leave at once, Mrs. Ellis."

"But it's Christmas Eve, your lordship. Your guests are here."

"They're so busy they won't notice if I nip out for a bit."

Frederick glanced around to be certain that indeed his guests would not notice his temporary absence. When no one seemed to pay him the slightest attention he disappeared upstairs to change and consider his next steps.

MRS. ELLIS WAS ABOUT to return downstairs to see if Mrs. Graham was still conscious. The housekeeper was stopped by an inquisitive stare from her husband, who had appeared as if out of the air, as he so often did.

"Where is his lordship going on Christmas Eve?" Mr. Ellis asked.

"I'm sure I don't know. It seemed important, though."

"Should I ask why you brought him that letter instead of me?"

"No, Mr. Ellis. You shouldn't."

"Very well." Again, the inquisitive stare, this time over the top of his spectacles. "This is highly unusual, I must say. His

CHRISTMAS AT HEMBRY CASTLE

lordship would never leave his guests at his own Christmas Eve celebration."

"I'm sure it was nothing more than some complaint from her ladyship, who is currently holding state in the drawing room, her ear trumpet pressed to the side of her head as she listens to the gossip from Lady Someone."

Mr. Ellis nearly laughed aloud but caught himself. Mrs. Ellis shooed her husband away.

"Go on. There's still so much to see to for the rest of the night."

Mr. Ellis nodded, gave his wife one more hard stare, and moved on.

POPPY FARM

*F*rederick, still dressed in his holiday finery, his red and green embroidered waistcoat a bright contrast to his black and white evening wear, grabbed his longest, heaviest overcoat, his thickest scarf, and his black leather fur-lined gloves. When Feesbury arrived to help, Frederick shooed him away. Frederick knew what he was doing was highly improper, to leave one's guests, on Christmas Eve no less. But the chatting and the laughter continued, and now people were shouting to be heard over the music and the stomps of the country dances that never seemed to end. The sight through the window brought a smile to Frederick's lips. Hembry had indeed become a winter wonderland. He would have stayed there to watch the simple joys that nature could bestow, but he had business to tend to, important business, and he must be on his way.

As soon as Frederick stepped outside he gasped. Snow was pleasant enough from the inside, but outside the air slapped his face with its briskness. He could have called on Perkins to drive him to the farms, but the outdoor staff had already started their holiday celebrations and they deserved this time to themselves. Frederick walked toward the stables then stopped. Whichever poor horse he chose would freeze nearly to its death. That, and the ground felt slippery under Frederick's boots so the animal would have to pick its steps gingerly. No, Frederick thought, I'll walk.

He took a moment to admire the winking stars, so clear through the cold Frederick thought he could touch them. He was certain he spotted the Christmas star, the one flashing the brightest. He walked along the paved path toward the tree-lined road that led to and from the castle, lost in the simple beauty of this Christmas Eve, the snow spread before him like a welcoming blanket. He stopped where the path ended. Yes, he could continue following the paved path, but the unpaved path was the shorter route to the farms. He chose the shorter route.

Frederick stepped off the pavement and there was nothing beneath his boots but slick, wet snow. He wondered how far he could go before he had to worry about frostbite or catching his death of cold. He looked again toward the path, thought again of Perkins and the stables, but decided no, I'm needed and I should get there as quickly as I can. I'm man enough to tough this out. It's only a little cold. This is England, after all.

He continued stubbornly forward, his toes now icicles in his boots. He should have put on his heavier hosiery, and he should have taken his walking stick, but it was too late to turn back now. He attempted to take his mind off his icy troubles by recalling the many pleasant Christmases he spent at Hembry in his youth. All the dancing and carols and meals and guests. He had loved the holidays when he was younger, the yellow of the candles, before gaslight, you know, and the orange from the hearth fires.

Richard and he would run through the rooms, wanting to

partake in all the festivities at once, wishing to speak to every person, sing every song, dance every dance, eat every bite, and drink as much hot buttered rum as their father allowed. Jumped up by sugar, butter, rum, spices, and whipped cream, Frederick and Richard ran faster, sang louder, and danced in dizzying circles. Everyone, with the exception of their mother, encouraged them, they were such spritely little boys, weren't they? Where was Jerrold all those times, Frederick wondered? All these years later, he still didn't know. Or care, particularly. How sad, that one should care so little for one brother and so much for the other, and the one I cared for is gone to Heaven. Richard had his problems, certainly. Frederick wouldn't hide from that difficult fact. When he was the Earl of Staton, Richard was gone from Hembry more than he was in residence at Hembry. But Richard was a good man with a good heart who only ever meant to do the right thing, even if he didn't always quite do it.

And then, for Richard to end in that horrible way, falling from a bridge in a drunken stupor. Mist blurred Frederick's vision, but he fought it, thinking that if his eyes became wet now his lids would freeze together. Instead, he became indignant. Why didn't Richard learn to swim, damn him? I offered to teach him, Pappa offered to teach him, Mamma offered to hire someone to teach him. Frederick caught himself. Even if Richard knew how to swim, would that have saved him, falling from that height, intoxicated, and not in command of himself? Likely, it would not have helped.

Without meaning to, determined to press the ugly thoughts aside but failing, Frederick remembered the horror-filled day when he had to identify his brother's remains at the morgue. It was like being in a dungeon, the darkness, the bodies on piles of straw, the suffocating stench of decay. When Frederick saw his brother's corpse he would have wept but he was too stunned. He had no doubt that he looked at his brother's remains. It was his brother's clothing, his brother's pocket watch, his brother's shirt pin, and there was that half-moon scar on his brother's temple. Yes, his brother had been disfigured beyond recognition by the fall, but Frederick would know his brother anywhere. That lifeless wax-like figure was indeed his beloved eldest brother passed too soon into eternity.

Frederick buckled over, praying that he didn't topple into the snowbank. With his hands on his knees, he heaved until he thought he would vomit. When the spasms settled he grabbed a handful of snow and rubbed it across his face and the back of his neck. His face and neck were now frozen into blocks of ice, but at least the wave of nausea passed. After taking another moment to breathe he continued toward the farms.

I have lost almost everyone I have ever loved, Frederick thought. Diana. Pappa. Richard. My dearest Daphne is heartbroken though she won't confide in me. She puts on a brave front, but I know she's hurting.

Suddenly, he heard a noise and stopped. It sounded like footsteps behind him. When Frederick heard nothing more he decided it must have been his own frozen feet pounding the icy ground. He pressed forward but stopped again when he heard an "Aaah!" as though someone had tripped. And then an "Achoo!" as if the very snow had sneezed. Again, silence. Frederick shook his head. I'm so chilled I'm hearing imaginary men sneezing and slipping across the ice, he thought.

He pulled his scarf closer, wishing now he had heeded Feesbury's offer of help. Feesbury would have found his warmest clothing, hosiery, and boots. Feesbury would have made sure he had help getting to the farms. Frederick shook his head. I'm a grown man with a grown daughter who is engaged to be married. Have I become so enfeebled since becoming earl that I've forgotten how to dress myself? He shook his head. It seems, sadly, that I have.

When the snow became sleet Frederick sighed. He had no umbrella either, and he was certain Feesbury would have thought of that as well. No matter. He was so wet he couldn't get any wetter, but so far as he could tell he was none the worse for it. A warm fire, dry clothing, and some hot tea should cure these ills. This is England, after all.

Frederick headed down the steep hill and nearly tripped as his ankles wobbled beneath him. His boots were heavy as he slogged through the muddy ground. He managed somehow to make it to the bottom in one piece. That's something, at least. Now in the village proper he passed the doctor's, the post office, the little vicarage with its little vicar who had served Frederick's grandfather. Frederick trod carefully along the winding road fit for a toboggan ride. He wished he had a toboggan. Under the moonlight the cottages were a sight to behold with their slanting gable roofs covered in a thick layer of snow, their white brick exteriors and white dusted shrubbery blending stoically into the winter scene while the nine-paned windows glowed with hearth fires. Frederick stepped gingerly across a thin, frozen pond, careful not to lose his footing. He was determined to make it to the farms with his extremities intact.

Finally, and not a moment too soon, he saw a checkerboard of properties that looked gray under the stormy nighttime sky. Then, with a bang! rain fell from what must have been upside down buckets in the sky. Soaked to his very bones, Frederick arrived at the door of Poppy Farm and knocked.

Mrs. Clayton's open eyes and wide mouth betrayed her shock. "Your lordship? Whatever brings you here?"

"I came straight away, Mrs. Clayton. Have you heard from your husband? I had a suspicion he was up to no good, though

I never could have guessed it was something as dreadful as this. Are you well? And what of your children?"

"But how did you know?"

"I received your note this evening."

Mrs. Clayton's open eyes closed in confusion.

"Did you not send for me?" Frederick asked.

"I haven't sent for anyone, your lordship. I certainly never sent for you. I would never trouble you with such a thing."

"With such a thing? When you're so in need of assistance?"

Frederick pulled his overcoat closer in an attempt to keep the water away but it was too late. He could feel his blood shivering in his veins.

"Come in, your lordship. You're soaked through." Mrs. Clayton pulled a simple chair before the hearth. "Please, dry yourself. You'll freeze to your death in this weather." Frederick nodded his appreciation and sat before the high, hot fire. "Forgive the mess, your lordship." Mrs. Clayton gestured at the home that looked perfectly tidy to Frederick's eyes, but he nodded, wishing to make the woman at ease in his presence, which she clearly was not.

"Would you like some tea, your lordship? It might help to warm the wet away."

"Only if it's no trouble, Mrs. Clayton."

She was a small woman, Mrs. Clayton, plump and pretty in her simple gingham dress under a homespun woolen jumper. As she busied herself with the tea things, Frederick held his hands out to the fire. It was quiet, too quiet for a house with five young children.

"And the children are...?" Frederick asked.

"With my neighbors," Mrs. Clayton said. "I asked them to take the children for a bit so I could pull myself together. I don't want to fall to pieces in front of them. I can't..." She

CHRISTMAS AT HEMBRY CASTLE

exhaled loudly. "I don't want the children to know. I won't say anything bad about their father in front of them."

"That's very good of you, Mrs. Clayton. You and your children are our first priority right now."

Mrs. Clayton pulled a coarse woolen sleeve to her eyes to wipe the streaks away. "It's good of you to inquire after us, your lordship, but we're not any of your concern, surely."

"If you are not my concern, then whose concern might you be? You are my tenant. Your husband, when he was worthy of the title, farmed my land. As the Earl of Staton, I'm responsible for the well being of those who live here. It's what my father believed, and his father believed, back to the time of Her Majesty Queen Elizabeth who created the title for my forebear."

Mrs. Clayton wept freely now. Her hands clasped the wood table before her as if it were the only thing holding her up.

"There there, Mrs. Clayton. All will be well. After we're certain that you and your children are cared for, our next job is to find that scoundrel husband of yours and get him to divorce you."

"Don't call him a scoundrel, your lordship. He's waylaid is all."

"Waylaid? I would use another word, but as you wish. Now." Frederick sipped his tea and studied the simply furnished room. "What do you need?"

"What I need, your lordship, is to return to my mother's. I don't want to live here any more. There are too many painful memories with my husband gone. This house is my nightmare now. It feels like a prison. I don't mean to offend your lordship."

"No offense taken, Mrs. Clayton. I understand you perfectly. I remember when Hembry Castle felt like a prison to

MEREDITH ALLARD

me." Frederick stopped himself. He had to focus on Mrs. Clayton. "Where does your mother live?"

"In Yorkshire, but with my husband gone..." She turned red, but Frederick nodded, encouraging her. "I haven't any money, your lordship. Not even enough to buy bread to feed my children."

"You needn't worry about a thing, Mrs. Clayton. You'll have plenty to eat and I'll take care of the passage for you and your children whenever you're ready. If you want to be with your mother in Yorkshire then in Yorkshire with your mother you shall be. When would you like to leave?"

"As soon as possible, my lord."

"Tomorrow is Christmas day. How about in three days? Will that give you enough time to prepare yourself and the children?"

"If it can be managed, your lordship, us leaving so soon."

"Very well then. In three days you'll be on the train to Yorkshire if that is your wish." Frederick thought of Clayton's apple face and sighed. "I am sorry it's ending this way, Mrs. Clayton. My greatest wish for you is for things to become easier as soon as possible. I believe they will, with time and healing. And even if you don't want to call him a scoundrel, what he did to you, abandoning you and your children as he has, well, I know it doesn't feel like it now, but in time I hope you'll see that you're better off without him."

Frederick could think of nothing more to say to Mrs. Clayton that might help her. He was nearly dry now and thought it best to take his leave. He stopped near the door.

"Mrs. Clayton, tomorrow is Christmas. You'll spend the day with us, won't you? I'd like your children to have a happy Christmas before they leave so at least they'll have one pleasant memory of Hembry."

92

"We could never do such a thing, your lordship, Christmas at the big house."

"I'm sorry, Mrs. Clayton, but I must insist. Lady Daphne would insist as well if she were here. Our public celebration is tonight, but tomorrow is a private, quiet day with the family. Everyone would be happy to have you and the children, I assure you."

"I think the children would enjoy it, your lordship. They're always asking to see the castle."

"Then do come, Mrs. Clayton. Be there at ten in the morning. We have our luncheon at noon."

"If your lordship insists."

"I do."

Mrs. Clayton smiled. "Then we'll gladly accept your invitation. Thank you."

"Very good. I'll send two of our maids over to pack whatever you wish to bring with you to Yorkshire. I'll send our carriage for you the morning of your departure."

Mrs. Clayton, forgetting all manner of propriety, grabbed Frederick's coat sleeve and tugged until he turned her way.

"You're a good man, your lordship, to concern yourself with us. Too many folks nowadays don't care a jot about others, only about themselves. Folks don't care who's kicked out of their home, who's ill, who's hurting, who's starving, who's dying. You're a rare blessing, your lordship, I mean it, I truly do. I hope the people of Hembry know what they have in you."

Frederick, afraid of an unmanly show of emotion, nodded his gratitude. He made his way outside and breathed in the sharp cold. The rain had stopped and the sky was a flat gray, the stars barely visible. He remembered the holiday festivities at the castle and wondered if anyone realized yet that he had gone. I should have told Daphne I was leaving, he thought, but then he remembered that Mrs. Ellis knew what had happened. As he left he noticed a two-wheeled governess cart pulled by a bored brown horse wearing a flowered quilt. The horse jolted to a stop before Poppy Farm. Frederick stopped too, waiting to see who was driving since her face was hidden under the fur-lined hood of her cloak. The woman was having trouble lifting herself from the tub-like seat, so he went to offer his assistance. When she looked up he remembered her, vividly.

"Why, Mrs. Gibson. It is you, isn't it?"

Mrs. Gibson was every bit as pretty as Frederick remembered. Dark hair, dark eyes, soft peaches and cream complexion.

"Yes, it's me," she said.

"Of course. I'd remember you anywhere." Frederick cleared his throat. He noticed her emerald green dress under her heavy cloak. "Are you no longer in mourning for your husband?"

"Yes, that's right. The mourning has ended."

"I see. And how are your children? I hope this holiday season isn't too difficult for them without their father."

"They're still getting used to life without him, but we're all doing better now, I think. That is kind of you to remember. Your lordship. Forgive me, I had forgotten that you're the Earl of Staton now. When we met you were the Earl of Staton's brother. You must still miss him as well."

"Very much so, especially tonight, I'm afraid. My brother did love Christmas." He heard that sound again, like footsteps on wet ground. "Did you hear that?"

"I did. Perhaps we're being followed. Perhaps it's a ghost." Mrs. Gibson laughed as she reached for the wicker basket beside her. "Tonight is a good night for ghosts. It is Christmas Eve, after all. Perhaps some kindly spirit will show us our lives, past, present, and future."

"Indeed. May I be of assistance?"

"I wouldn't want to put you out, your lordship."

"Nothing of the sort. Please." Frederick took her wicker basket in one hand and offered his other, which Mrs. Gibson accepted. With Frederick's support she climbed out of the governess cart and steadied herself on the slippery ground.

"What are you doing here, your lordship?" Mrs. Gibson asked. "This is far from the holiday entertainments at Hembry Castle."

"I received a note this evening that Mrs. Clayton's husband abandoned her for some tart in London and she and the children were left destitute this Christmas. I couldn't have that, now, could I, so I came directly."

"Mrs. Clayton sent me the same note. I'm so glad she thought to reach out to us. Whenever I've come across her in the village she always seemed so self-reliant I didn't think she was the kind who would ask for help if her life depended on it."

"That's the thing. It turns out it wasn't Mrs. Clayton who sent the note. She said she hasn't contacted anyone."

"Not anyone?"

"She seemed genuinely surprised to see me, as I suspect she will be when she sees you."

Mrs. Gibson took the basket from Frederick. "I brought some food and treats so she and the children can have a nice Christmas. I slipped some money into the basket so she'll be all right for a while. I'm happy to help her with whatever she needs."

"That's very kind of you, Mrs. Gibson. In fact, Mrs. Clayton has decided to return to her mother in Yorkshire and I'm certain the money and the food will be much appreciated. She's spending Christmas with us at the castle."

"Then she's certain to have a happy Christmas." Mrs.

Gibson looked at the cottage. "So who contacted us, do you think?"

"I really couldn't say."

Mrs. Gibson shivered as a brisk wind blew past.

"You should get inside where it's warm," Frederick said, "and I should get back home." Mrs. Gibson nodded, lingered a moment, then walked toward the door. Before she knocked Frederick called, "And what about you and the children, Mrs. Gibson? Would you like to spend Christmas at Hembry Castle? We'd so like to have you. I know Lady Daphne would be thrilled to see you again. Your children will have other children to play with when Mrs. Clayton comes, and my young nephew will be there as well."

"I wouldn't want to trouble you with more guests, your lordship."

"You could never be any trouble to me."

Even in the dark, Frederick was certain she blushed, and it was an attractive blush indeed.

"I would be happy to accept your generous invitation, Lord Staton."

"Come at ten in the morning. We have luncheon at noon."

"We'll be there. Thank you."

Frederick tipped his hat toward the pretty widow. He stayed back as he watched Mrs. Gibson knock to be welcomed by a wide eyed Mrs. Clayton. When both women were inside, Frederick made his way past the stretch of farmland toward the road that led back to the castle. The cold passed over him now that he had so much to think about.

What had just happened? He had helped someone who needed him, and Frederick admitted that it was a good feeling, to do something good for someone, especially this time of year. Mrs. Clayton was so surprised that he had taken the time to help her. But what else was he to do? She needed help so he helped her.

Frederick looked at the opalescent sky and wondered if it would snow again. It must be Christmas by now, certainly. How many guests thought him ill-mannered for not being there to bid his adieus? But he was certain Daphne and his mother had made his excuses for him. Frederick was happy for the walk back to the castle since it allowed him time to think.

Perhaps there was some logic in his becoming the Earl of Staton after all. Perhaps this was his calling, or, if not his calling, since his brother should still be alive, but perhaps this is what he is meant to do now that Richard is no longer here. My job is to help people. Yes, Frederick thought. I want to help people. And as earl I have the means through which to do that.

Frederick realized that he wanted to do his best to fix things, change things, make life better and more comfortable for everyone at Hembry. And when better to learn that lesson than the Christmas season when people wanted to make merry while feeling they did some good in this world?

And then there was the pretty widow. Well, Frederick thought, grinning. We'll see how it goes tomorrow and take it from there.

THAT BOY

*E*dward Ellis sat alone in his Fetter Lane flat watching the snowflakes fall like lace to the ground. He felt heavy, as though he were tethered down by a sadness he had never known before, and he had seen some troubles in his day. He couldn't write, he couldn't sleep, he couldn't concentrate. His work at the Observer was suffering. At the moment he was hungry, but walking across the room to see if there was anything to eat was too much for him, so he sat, and he sat some more.

He was lonely, certainly. It was Christmas Eve and he was sat there by himself lost in pain-filled thoughts. He longed for the comfortable warmth of Hembry Castle with Daphne by his side. He dropped his head into his hands as he thought of Daphne, how he had avoided her, afraid of telling her the truth. He knew how much he hurt her, and that's what tortured him most of all. But he had no words. That was the root of his problems. His words were gone. His Christmas story never materialized. He had been released by his publishers and no longer deserving of the title of author. He had no money to support his future wife. He was the son of a spendthrift. He was in all ways a failure. And yet he missed Daphne so much. It was a physical ache, missing her. Certainly, she was over him by now. She could do so much better. Perhaps that duke's heir Daphne's grandmother had wanted for her was still searching for a wife.

Edward remembered last year when he had spent Christmas at Hembry Castle. He loved the festivities, the joy, the music, the spiced punch. Mainly, he loved Daphne. Christmas at Hembry Castle was nothing new to him. He had often spent his Christmases there when he was a boy, downstairs with the servants while his grandparents supervised the celebrations. When no one was watching he would sneak bites of cakes and sips of eggnog, often wondering how the footmen carried the drinks upstairs, the delicate glasses teetering precariously on silver trays, when the footmen could hardly keep themselves upright after furtive gulps of mulled wine. Edward's heart shattered like a dropped glass at the knowledge that he would never have a Christmas like that again. He would never have Daphne again.

When his back ached from sitting in the same position too long he stretched his arms toward the ceiling. He shivered, then realized that the fire in the hearth had nearly died away. He struck the lingering flames with the stick but instead he extinguished whatever little heat remained. He stared at the wisps of smoke as though hoping for some magical fix to all his problems. He was startled by a loud banging at his door.

"Edward!" a man's voice called. "Edward Ellis, you must come!"

Edward didn't recognize the voice. He pulled open the door but there was no one. He walked down the hall this way and the other way but still there was no one. He went downstairs and asked the landlady who had been there. When she said there were no visitors that night Edward went back inside his rooms, shaking his head at his own foolishness. Then he heard it again, a banging at his door.

"Edward Ellis, where are you? You must come straight away!"

This time Edward flung his door open so hard it bounced off the wall, but still the hall was empty. He looked to the right and saw a man's top hat disappearing down the stairs. Edward grabbed the first coat he saw, the first hat, and he pulled both on as he raced down the stairs trying to catch the man as he ran through the front door and down the street.

"Wait!" Edward called. "Who are you? What do you want?"

Edward ran after the man, or he tried. The snow had turned to sleet and the ground was freezing beneath his feet, leaving the road too slippery to move too quickly without losing his balance as well as his sight on the man. Edward had to stop himself twice from hitting the ground face-first. The top hat, along with the man wearing it, turned down this alley and that road. There were others out and about that bone-chilling night, it was Christmas Eve after all, and people turned confused stares onto Edward, who was clearly tipsy to their eyes. Edward didn't mind them. He had to know what this man wanted.

After one last corner Edward found himself alone. The man in the top hat had disappeared. Had he been chasing some poor soul for no reason, Edward wondered? Was that even the same man who had knocked on his door? Was there even a knock on his door? He didn't know. He rubbed his hands together, realizing he had no gloves. He blew into his hands, which didn't help since his breath was cold. He looked around, trying to gauge his surroundings. Then he felt snow on his face. He caught one snowflake on his finger and pulled it close, examining the exquisite design. How perfect nature is, he thought. Something as tiny as a snowflake and look at the crystalline beauty.

Hearty laughter and carol singing emanated from the homes surrounding him and he remembered it was Christmas Eve. Suddenly, he felt very much alone in the world. He looked once more for the gentleman in the top hat but this part of the road was deserted. He was the only one outside in the snow. All right then, Edward thought. I have not only lost my words, I have lost my mind.

"Edward?"

Edward knew the speaker before he turned around. It was his very own sister, Kate, looking rather like a Christmas doll in her green dress, white cloak, white fur hat, and white muffle.

Edward laughed. "Was it you? Did you lure me here, dear sister?"

"I thought you lured me here."

Kate showed Edward the note written in a hand he didn't recognize. He glanced across the street, hoping yet again to catch some glimpse of the man in the top hat.

"Why would someone bring us both here?" Edward said. "Why on earth…" He stopped as he realized where they stood —on Theobalds Road near Grays Inn.

"What is it, Neddie?"

Edward gestured to the well-tended brick home across the road. "This is Christina Chattaway's house."

"Maybe there's something here we need to see," Kate said.

"What could I possibly need to see at the house of the woman I used to be engaged to? Is someone trying to get back at me by reminding me how much pain I caused Christina when I broke off our engagement?"

Kate's face flushed with cold or excitement or both. "Let's see."

"No, Kate. I..."

But Kate was already crossing the street, lifting her hems just enough that they wouldn't soak through as she bounded across the slick puddles. Edward followed behind. He narrowly missed being hit by a coach driver who shook his fist and shouted words Edward hoped his sister hadn't heard. Kate drew close to the Chattaways' window and peered in. The blood red brocade curtains were pulled back, revealing a happy holiday celebration inside. Edward and Kate hid themselves behind a wet, drooping hedge.

"You know what his reminds me of?" Kate asked.

"Don't say it. I can't bear to think of Christmas stories right now."

Kate said nothing but she smiled. The window to the Chattaways' home was cracked open enough to allow some fresh air into the room, so brother and sister stopped talking. Edward watched the Christmas party play out like a spot of brightness on this bleak winter night. Some crowded around the refreshment table drinking large helpings of mulled cider. Some danced. Some sang.

"There's Christina," Kate whispered.

She had always been a pretty girl, Christina. Plump, pale-skinned, and pale-haired, a sweet smile for anyone she spoke to. But after Edward met Daphne his heart lit up in a way he hadn't known possible. He liked Christina very much, and he even loved her in a way, but Christina didn't understand him as Daphne did. Christina was sweet and nice but not particularly inquisitive. She wasn't interested in his writing beyond asking when he would be finished so they could spend time together. But when they did spend time together she never had much to say. And then Daphne arrived from America, and from the moment Edward saw her he knew what it was to have light in your life, to have color and music and everything good.

"What have I done?"

Kate grabbed her brother's arm, a growing panic on her face. "You're not regretting breaking things off with Christina, are you?"

"No, it's just that I can see now that I've been a fool to stay away from Daphne. Daphne is the only woman for me. She has given me my life. She has given me hope, and air, and music, and joy, and I've been ignoring her because I couldn't tell her... I couldn't tell her..."

"I know, Neddie. But it's not too late. She loves you. She misses you."

"How do you know?"

"Grandmother told me. There's still time, but you must make it up to her and soon."

If Edward could have kicked his own backside he would have.

"No more," he said. "Father will affect me no more."

"That's right, Neddie. Go to Hembry Castle, tell Lady Daphne everything, and set a date for the wedding. Please."

Through the window Edward noticed Thomas Roberts, one of the journalists from the Daily Observer, hovering near Christina Chattaway. Thomas leaned his dark head toward Christina's fair head and she looked up at him, shyly, as they spoke. The way Mrs. Chattaway beamed at the two young people made Edward wonder.

"Look at them," Kate said. "Do you think they're engaged?"

"I hope they are. He's a good man, Roberts. He's even-tempered, stable, reliable, like Christina. He's far better for her than I ever would have been. They're perfect for one another. I hope they're very happy."

"And I hope you and Lady Daphne will be very happy."

Edward smiled for the first time in what felt like an eternity. He took his sister's arm and led her away from the window, leaving the Chattaways to celebrate with friends and family. They had moved on, and so had he.

Edward and Kate made their way down the street in silence. The night had grown busier and people were out paying calls in honor of the holiday.

"Let me take you back to Barking," Edward said.

"I'm spending Christmas with my friend Ellen and her family. They're just around the corner."

Edward walked his sister to the house she indicated.

"Won't you come in for some tea to warm yourself before you go home?"

Edward saw the shadow of a woman, likely Ellen's mother, pass the open window. "Not tonight. Tonight I have to think about what I want to say to Daphne."

"And you'll tell Ma and Pa?"

Edward exhaled and cold smoke framed his face. "I'll speak to them. But first I have to speak to Daphne."

"Of course." Kate kissed her brother's cheek. "Send me a telegram when everything is settled. I don't want you coming back from Hembry without a wedding date, do you hear me?"

"I do."

He watched his sister knock on her friend's house and waited until she was inside. He practically slid back to Fetter Lane, the ground was so icy now. As he slid he wondered. Who had banged on his door and beckoned him? Who sent the note to Kate? And why lead them both to Christina's? Whatever the intention, he was certain that Daphne was all that mattered to him. His life wasn't worth living without her.

CHRISTMAS AT HEMBRY CASTLE

*D*aphne stood near the white stone hearth warming her hands. She scanned the burgundy Queen Anne furniture, the burgundy and blue rugs, the portraits on the walls. Then she watched the footmen remove the candles from the tree, light them, and nestle them back into the branches. That was always her favorite part of the holiday, the glowing tree. There was something comforting about the greenery, the decorations, and the lights even if she wasn't feeling particularly merry this Christmas.

Christmas morning was quiet, which Daphne appreciated after a night of hundreds of guests. Daphne and her father shared a simple breakfast, just the two of them since her grandmother took her breakfast in bed. Her father's face was bright as he described the events from the night before. Daphne hadn't seen her father so excited about anything in a long while and it made her happy to see it.

"Do you like Mrs. Gibson?" Daphne asked. Frederick said nothing, but his grin revealed everything.

"I'm glad," Daphne said. "I like her too. Hembry Castle

could use some more life around here. Some young children would brighten things up nicely."

Frederick scoffed. "It's far too soon for that, young lady. For now, let's say I'm glad that I've had the opportunity to renew my acquaintance with Mrs. Gibson."

"But what about Mrs. Clayton, Papa? Surely there must be more we can do for her and her children."

Frederick shoveled another forkful of eggs and bacon into his mouth, washing it down with some tea. "For now, her dearest wish is to return to her mother in Yorkshire so that's where she shall go. After that, we'll consider what she needs and take it from there."

Daphne watched her father take another hearty bite of his meal while her fried potatoes grew cold on her plate.

"What is it, Daphne?"

"I was just wondering about her husband. How could he do such a thing?"

"I wish I knew."

Mr. Ellis refilled Daphne's tea cup before she thought to ask. "Do you think he has another woman?"

"I'm afraid he does. But at least I've solved one problem at Hembry."

"There will always be problems at Hembry, Papa. That's the nature of being the earl."

"I think I've finally come to accept that. I had some important realizations last night. Some important realizations, indeed." Frederick dabbed at his lips with his napkin while Ellis whisked his empty plate away. "I've been fighting being the Earl of Staton since your uncle died. I thought it was a cruel trick that he died when he did, with so much life ahead of him. I thought it was unfair that he left me with this burden. But then I remembered how he died, and I realized that instead of feeling bullied by fate I should be thankful for all of this." He gestured at the luxurious surroundings of the castle, then kissed Daphne's hand. "And I am thankful for you, my most darling daughter. I'm thankful for all of it, even if I didn't understand what any of it meant at first. Last night, seeing how Mrs. Clayton needed me, knowing that I could assist her in some small way, it helped me realize that I do have a place here. I know other problems are on the horizon and the people of Hembry will always need me and I want to be here for them."

"I'm so glad to hear you say it, Papa. But you've come to this conclusion before."

"I've come to this conclusion a few times since your uncle died, but this time it feels right, as if I'm not just saying the words. This time I feel it in my bones. I don't know how else to explain it. I see my purpose now. I'll have to take it day by day, but I believe I can make a go of it, Daphne. I believe everything will be all right."

"What about the falling harvest prices? What will you do about that?"

"For now we've managed without much of a decline in our profits and we'll be fine this year. As for next year? Well, my darling, we'll figure it out. For now, let's leave aside any worries. Today is Christmas, after all. We have guests on their way, and I say let's enjoy the day."

"I'm so proud of you, Papa. And I'm glad we're having some guests to celebrate with us. It will help keep my mind off things."

"What things, Daphne?" Frederick looked so earnest, and Daphne loved him dearly for it. But she only shook her head. She wouldn't burden him now, especially not when he looked so pleased. She noticed Mrs. Ellis hovering near the open door.

"Yes, Mrs. Ellis?"

"I'm sorry to disturb you, Lady Daphne, but you're wanted in the library."

"Is something wrong?"

"Come see for yourself, my lady."

Daphne looked at her father, who shrugged in response. She followed Mrs. Ellis down the hallway, around a corner, and down another hallway and another corner. There were still days when Daphne lost her way along the labyrinth halls and serpentine staircases. They passed the hall of ancestors, as her father called them, generations of Meriwethers smiling or smirking or grimacing as the mood struck them.

"I still think their eyes follow me wherever I go," Daphne said.

"I've been here a long time, my lady, and I feel the same."

"You won't tell me what it is, Mrs. Ellis?"

"It's a surprise."

"A good one?"

"I certainly hope so, my lady."

Mrs. Ellis opened the library door and Daphne saw Edward near the window. He bowed when he saw her.

"Lady Daphne Meriwether," he said, "thank you for seeing me this beautiful Christmas morning."

Daphne looked at Mrs. Ellis, hoping for some sign of what this was about, but Mrs. Ellis kept her housekeeper's mask on, revealing nothing, shutting the door behind her.

Edward hopped from one foot to the next like he had ants in his pants, Daphne thought, as he poured them both a toddy from the bowl on the side table. His hand shook as he ladled the hot drink into the cups. Daphne breathed in the ruby red port, the nutmeg, the ginger, and allowed the warmth to comfort her.

"Am I going to need this?" she asked.

110

"Perhaps. It depends on how you react to what I have to say."

Daphne took a small sip. The heat from the alcohol and the sugar filled her with strength. If it was time to have things out with Edward then it was time. She set her drink on the table and waited. Edward returned to the window, watching the heavy snowfall stick to the ground.

"Snow on Christmas," Daphne said. "Normally I would say it's good luck."

"And today?"

"I'm not so sure today."

Edward nodded. He drank down the toddy in one long gulp then poured himself another and had that one down just as quick. Finally, he turned to Daphne. His long chocolate-colored hair fell on either side of his boyish face, his hazel eyes wide as always, taking in everything at once. He stared at Daphne, hard, as though trying to read her, read all of her. She stayed silent as she waited.

"All right then," Edward said. "Here goes." He sat beside Daphne and took her hand. "First, my darling, I want to apologize with all my heart. I know I've been distant toward you, and you are the last person in the world I ever want to be distant from. You are my everything. You must know that."

"Then what is it? Do you not want to marry me, Edward? Because if you don't want to get married…"

"I want to marry you more than I want anything else in this world."

"Then what won't you tell me?"

A gentle knock rattled the door. Edward's grandfather showed Frederick into the room then shut the door behind him.

"What is it?" Frederick asked. "Is everything all right between you?"

"No," Edward said, "I mean, yes. I mean, everything will be all right. I hope."

"Should I leave? Ellis said I was wanted, but do you two need to speak alone?"

"It's better that you're both here. I should tell you both at the same time."

"Please, Edward," Daphne said. "Tell me."

So he did. Edward told them everything. About his father's carelessness with money, how he begged, borrowed, or stole until he hadn't a friend in the world, how his grandparents bailed him out but now they no longer would, or so they said. He talked until he hadn't anything left to say on any subject ever. He had finally found his words.

Daphne watched the beads of sweat form on Edward's upper lip as he spoke. When he finished he exhaled, then drank down one more steaming cup.

"That's why you avoided me? You were worried that I wouldn't want to marry you because of your father?"

"Think of it, Daphne, Your father is the Earl of Staton. Our son, should we be blessed with one, will be your father's heir. And all along my father will be sniffing around asking for a handout for this reason or that reason, sounding perfectly friendly all the time yet meaning to fleece you for every pound you're willing to hand over. Can you imagine that man as the grandfather of the heir to Hembry Castle?"

"This is what you've been hiding?" Frederick asked.

"That's the whole story. Or, that and I've been released from Fergusonandwately. I'm afraid I can no longer call myself an author."

Daphne helped herself to another steaming cup and took a long sip. "It will certainly be something to tell our children one day, how their father was so afraid to tell me the most simple thing. I can't believe you think so little of me that you believe something like that would put me off, Edward Augustus Ellis. I love you."

"Do you really?"

"Of course I do. And I understand now why it was so important to you to receive your payment from your publisher before we married and why it was such a problem for you not to finish the book. I see why you work yourself to the bone to pay your own way in the world. You're afraid if you're dependent on anyone, even my father, you wouldn't be any better than your own father, asking everyone for money and owing debts everywhere."

Edward bowed his head. "I will do right by you, Daphne. I promise."

"I know you will, Edward. You're not your father. You're the finest man I know. I trust you with my very life."

Frederick clasped Edward's shoulder. "You let your father try his best, young man. I believe I can handle him. And to relieve any worry on that point, I'm not concerned about the grandfather of the future Earl of Staton. My only concern is the father of the future Earl of Staton, and I can think of no one better than you, Edward. And if you and Daphne need some financial assistance before your author career flourishes again," Frederick held up a firm hand when Edward tried to protest, "then consider it a wedding present from a father-in-law who has no greater wish than his daughter's happiness. As Daphne said, you are not your father. You will make a success of whatever you put your mind to, and that above all else is what I want from the father of the future Earl of Staton."

"Besides," Daphne said, "if things work out between Papa and the pretty widow, as it seems they might, you may have a son after all, Papa."

"Nonsense!" But her father's face reddened to a certain shade of pomegranate and an impish grin played up his lips.

"I like Mrs. Gibson very much, Papa. I hope it does work out for you."

Edward knelt before Daphne. "I know how lucky I am in you, my love. I should have told you from the beginning. I can see that now." He turned to Frederick. "You did the right thing, sending me to Christina's last night to remind me how unhappy I would have been if I had married anyone but Daphne."

"Send you to Christina's? You mean the Chattaways? I didn't send you anywhere, Edward. I wasn't even sure what was wrong between you since Daphne didn't confide in me."

"You didn't come to my flat last night to lead me to Christina's? You didn't send the note to my sister so we'd meet on the way? I thought you must have realized that I would come to my senses if I saw Christina and was reminded of my time with her." Edward looked at Daphne. "Was it you?"

"It's a brilliant idea, Edward, but I'm afraid it wasn't me, either. Was it your grandparents?"

"No," Edward said. "The hand that wrote Kate's note didn't belong to either of them, and the person I chased to Christina's was too tall to be my grandfather and it was definitely a man."

"Mrs. Gibson and I also received notes from an anonymous source," Frederick said. "That's how we ended up at Poppy Farm at the same time. But honestly, I couldn't give two figs about any of that right now. You two are reconciled and that's all the holiday cheer I need. Edward," he took his future son-in-law by the arm, "you're family now, you know. Or we will be as soon as we have a wedding date settled. You will set a new date now, won't you? You don't have any other confessions for me, do you?"

"That's all I have to tell you," Edward said. "And as for the wedding date, the sooner the better, I say."

"Well, Daphne?" Frederick eyed his daughter, waiting.

Daphne thought her happiness was bright enough to light every candle in Hembry Castle. "The sooner the better, I say."

Edward kissed Daphne's hand. "Thank you, my love. That's what I needed to hear."

DAPHNE CHANGED for the intimate Christmas gathering in time to greet her guests. She wore a claret-colored dress with a pleated bodice and a high neck while her gathered overskirts emphasized the bustle at her back, setting her slim figure to great advantage, Edward thought. Her gold hair was swept high into a swirled coiffure with a single long curl dangling over her shoulder, emphasizing her heart-shaped face and amethyst eyes.

"I'm the most fortunate man in the world, Lady Daphne Meriwether."

"And I'm the most fortunate woman, Mr. Edward Ellis."

The guests arrived promptly at ten in the morning. First Mrs. Gibson and her two children arrived, a boy of five and a girl of three. Both children took after their mother, dark haired and dark eyed with bright smiles. Daphne saw her father watching Mrs. Gibson, watching the children, trying to see, she guessed, if he could imagine himself living with them and being happy. They were lovely children, Daphne thought, well behaved, polite, and full of good cheer. The children, Robert and Rose, oohed and aahed at the sight of the castle on full holiday display, the green pointed holly leaves with the blossoming red berries, the displays of ivy and rosemary, the tall trees in every room, the dishes of orange peel candies set on the low tables in easy reach of small hands. Then Mrs. Clayton arrived with her five young ones alongside Lucy Escott, a former maid for Daphne's Uncle Jerrold, and little Josiah, the result of Uncle Jerrold's, well, you know. With all of their guests present, Daphne and Edward brought the children into the sitting room where a bare tree, short enough for the children to reach, was set up near the window. Daphne and Edward passed around boxes of ornaments, which the children giggled to see. The children sang "Deck the Halls" as they placed the paper-mache trinkets on the branches and created popcorn and candy strings to wrap from top to bottom.

Deck the halls with boughs of holly, Fa la la la la la la la!
Tis the season to be jolly, Fa la la la la la la la!
Don we now our gay apparel, Fa la la la la la la la!
Troll the ancient Yuletide carol, Fa la la la la la la la!
See the blazing yule before us, Fa la la la la la la la!
Strike the harp and join the chorus, Fa la la la la la la la!
Follow me in merry measure, Fa la la la la la la la!
While I tell of Yuletide treasure, Fa la la la la la la la!
Fast away the old year passes, Fa la la la la la la la!
Hail the new, ye lads and lasses, Fa la la la la la la la!
Sing we joyous all together! Fa la la la la la la la!
Heedless of the wind and weather, Fa la la la la la la la!

After the tree was decorated, Edward lit the candles and set them between the branches. Everyone, including Edward and Daphne, Frederick and Mrs. Gibson, Robert and Rose, Mrs. Clayton and her children, Lucy Escott and Josiah, the Ellises, and the maids and footmen cheered at the sight of the children's tree. Everyone watched as the footmen hauled in the yule log, set it in the center of the hearth, and lit it. The heavy chunk of wood, smelling of pine and cinnamon, burned bright orange until Frederick sprinkled some liquid over it and the log burned green and smelled of apples.

As the children continued to take pride in their very own tree, the footmen brought in trays of buttery tea biscuits, slices of gingerbread, and pots of steaming tea. Frederick, upon seeing the servants watching from the doorway, invited them to share a holiday treat.

"Today is Christmas," Frederick said. "Let's not stand on ceremony today."

Daphne stood back, watching. This was her gift. She had a family. She had a father she adored, a husband-to-be who she loved more than she ever knew was possible, and now she had grandparents. She had been missing her grandfather a lot lately, but knowing she had the Ellises helped ease the ache. Then Daphne realized. Her grandmother, the Countess of Staton, was not there with them.

Daphne guessed where her grandmother was hiding and made her way to the blue and white sitting room. She knocked on the door, and when she heard a faint response she went inside.

The Countess of Staton was not in her usual throne-like chair beside the fire. Instead, the grand old dame sat near the window watching the snow fall. Crystalline icicles froze on the bare tree branches, hanging between heaven and earth.

"It's beautiful, isn't it, Grandma?" Daphne asked.

"Indeed it is, Daphne."

She seemed lethargic, Lady Staton, odd since she always seemed so formidable. Emboldened by her grandmother's quiet demeanor, Daphne took her hand.

"Come, Grandma. Everyone is here for Christmas. Won't you celebrate with us?"

"Yes, the singing was so loud I could hear it without my ear trumpet."

"Then won't you come?"

"In a moment, my dear. I was just thinking of your Uncle Richard. He did so love the holidays. It was his favorite time of year. When he was a boy he'd walk through the castle reading A Christmas Carol aloud to anyone who would listen, and then when the holiday came he'd do everything in his power to celebrate just like it said in the book." The countess slumped forward, and Daphne was afraid her grandmother was ill. Lady Staton's mourning black made her look even more pale, as if her life force had seeped away.

"I worry, Daphne," Lady Staton said. "I worry that your grandfather and I were too hard on Richard. We knew he didn't want to be earl so we felt it was our duty to prepare him properly. But he was so troubled by it all, wasn't he? Do you think he blamed us?"

"Of course not, Grandma. I have no doubt he understood that you and Grandpa were trying to prepare him for what was coming when he became the earl."

"I wanted to be above reproach. I didn't want the wagging tongues of others to interfere in our lives. When he was Earl of Staton he was never here and I thought he was being irresponsible and I was hard on him then too. But he was a grown man, wasn't he, and I'm sure he hated having his mother meddle in his business." The Countess of Staton sighed. "If I could only do it again, Daphne, I would do it all so differently." Lady Staton, who had not removed her hand from Daphne's, now squeezed tightly. "When you have children, Daphne, let them find their own way. If people talk they talk. That's what I've learned, sitting here on my own since my son died. Maybe what others think is less important than how we treat our own family."

Daphne squeezed her grandmother's hand right back. When she saw her grandmother's eyes fill with tears, she had to fight back her own.

"We all miss Uncle Richard so much, Grandma. But I know he wouldn't want us sitting around feeling sad. He certainly wouldn't want you here alone while the rest of us are celebrating Christmas together."

Lady Staton nodded. She took up her ear trumpet from the wing chair, slipped the chain over her head, and patted the trumpet so it lay flat again her chest. She took Daphne's arm and accompanied her granddaughter to the great room where the children skipped and danced around the tree. The Countess of Staton, a stark figure in black against the glow of the green and red holiday, softened as she walked with Daphne.

"Who are these children?" Lady Staton asked.

"Some are from the farms. They're leaving for Yorkshire in a few days and Papa wanted them to have a nice Christmas before they left. Of course, you remember Lucy and Josiah. And the boy and girl near Papa belong to Mrs. Gibson."

"Mrs. Gibson? The widow?"

"That's right. Papa saw her at the farms yesterday and invited her and her children to spend the day with us."

Lady Staton's pale eyes brightened. "Well well. Well well. We may have more than one wedding to celebrate soon." She turned her sharp gaze onto Daphne. "Are you marrying Edward Ellis, then?"

"I am, Grandma. I'm sorry if that's a disappointment to you, but I love him dearly, and he loves me. There's no one else in the world for me, so I'm afraid we're stuck with him."

Daphne kissed her grandmother's cheek, and her grandmother, instead of being annoyed by her highly American display of affection, nodded her approval, which meant everything to Daphne. When they saw Frederick huddled in the corner, speaking intently to Mrs. Gibson, granddaughter and grandmother smiled.

Frederick called to everyone to join him in the library where the pantomime was ready to begin, and then he disappeared. The children sat before the large red velvet curtain hanging from a line from the ceiling. Everyone clapped when the curtain was pulled aside to reveal an improvised set for "Jack and the Beanstalk." Frederick was there, looking rather fine in farmer's attire—button down shirt, sack coat, denim overalls, and a straw hat, puffing on a cob pipe for good measure. When he called "Jack!" none other than Robert, Mrs. Gibson's son, came out from behind the curtain, shouting "Yessir!" for all the world to hear. When Edward appeared in a dress, speaking in a squeaking voice, and curtseying so low he could hardly stand again, Daphne screamed with laughter along with the children. There was something about this moment, the silliness of it, the joy of it, that made her heart swell. Seeing her future husband and her father playing together for everyone's entertainment, watching adorable little Robert forgetting his lines to have Frederick whisper them in his ear, laughing at Edward's slapstick as he tripped over every flat surface on the makeshift stage, all of it made Daphne grateful for everything that brought her to this moment with everyone she loved and those she would come to love soon enough, she was sure. This is Christmas, Daphne thought. This warmth, this togetherness, this love. This is what it's all about. And Daphne was grateful for all of it.

As Jack scampered away to climb the beanstalk, Lady Staton leaned close to Daphne.

"I know it's too late to help Richard, Daphne, but I will be here for you and that boy. I promise."

"I know, Grandma. Thank you."

With the pantomime complete and everyone in a jolly mood, Mrs. Ellis passed around peppermint sticks while everyone sang together.

God rest ye merry, gentlemen
Let nothing you dismay
Remember, Christ, our Saviour
Was born on Christmas day

To save us all from Satan's power
When we were gone astray
O tidings of comfort and joy,
Comfort and joy
O tidings of comfort and joy.

After the singing, Lady Staton sat down to the piano and played an upbeat waltz. Edward bowed to Daphne.

"May I sign my name to your dance card, Lady Daphne?"

"I don't have a dance card, Mr. Ellis. It's only family and friends here this fine Christmas day, and besides, I'm no longer in need of dance cards. I'm engaged, didn't you know? I'll be married soon."

"Whoever the man is, he is the most fortunate man ever to walk this earth." Edward extended his hand. "Lady Daphne, will you do me the honor of dancing with me?"

Daphne curtsied and took Edward's arm. He led her to the open space in the center of the great room, and soon they were joined by Frederick and Mrs. Gibson. Daphne noticed her grandmother watching them, Daphne and Edward and Frederick and Mrs. Gibson, looking happier than Daphne had ever seen her.

"Happy Christmas, my love," Edward said.

"Merry Christmas, Edward."

"Shall we set a date? I think everyone here would think it was the greatest gift of all if we set a wedding date."

"April," Daphne said. "Spring weddings are the most beautiful, after all."

"April it is. And I cannot wait."

Edward led Daphne to the refreshment table and handed her a glass of mulled wine. He nodded toward the Earl of Staton and Mrs. Gibson, still waltzing and laughing the entire time.

"Will he marry her, do you think?"

"I hope so," Daphne said.

CHRISTMAS LUNCHEON WAS SERVED. Her ladyship, in consultation with Lady Daphne and Mrs. Graham, decided on a casual meal where the feast was set out on a long sideboard in the great room for everyone to enjoy as they pleased during breaks between dancing and games. Mr. and Mrs. Ellis were invited guests as part of the family, but the servants were invited to enjoy as they wished. This was Christmas, after all.

Golden roast beef, roast chicken, roast duck, and roast goose sat alongside quail with truffles, fermety with almonds, saffron, and cinnamon, green salads, oysters, beef consommé, bread stuffing, scalloped potatoes, and bite-sized minced pies, sweet potato pies, pork pies, beef pies, and more minced pies. At one end of a second sideboard sat pots of steaming tea, hot chocolate, wassail, mulled wine, hot gin punch, smoking bishop—which Edward made a point of ignoring—chocolate Christmas coffee, and negus for the children. At the other end were Christmas cakes with holly sprigs, sugar plums, buttery biscuits, figgy pudding, Stars of Bethlehem with pink icing, chocolate yule logs, iced gingerbread, spiced apple cakes, orange and chocolate scones, orange custard, and plum puddings with hard sauce.

Daphne took great joy in the children's delight as they tasted this a bit of an oyster and dove head first into that plum pudding. Someone stepped behind her, but she didn't need to turn to know who it was. Finally, he leaned close to the back of her neck. She wished he would kiss her.

"Well?" Edward said around a bite of iced gingerbread. "Who was it?"

"Who was what?"

"Who sent the notes to your father and the pretty widow to

CHRISTMAS AT HEMBRY CASTLE

lure them to the Claytons' farm? Who kept banging on my door and led me down the road, and who sent the note to Kate to get us to Christina's house at the same time?" He grinned. "Think about it, Daphne. Who else might it be?"

"No! He wouldn't risk being found out, not after he went to so much trouble to disappear." Daphne laughed so loudly everyone looked her way. She whispered in Edward's ear. "Do you really think it was him?"

"The man who led me from my flat was tall and lanky. It could have been him. Who else could have orchestrated such a perfect Christmas?"

Daphne watched her father in the act of putting a small slice of cake on a plate for little Rose. "If it was him, then I'm grateful. He brought us back together. He helped Papa find some peace, and Mrs. Gibson. This is indeed a perfect Christmas."

The Ellises, Augustus and Mary, were dancing to "The Twelve Days of Christmas" and doing it quite well.

"Has your grandmother said anything to you about him?" Daphne asked.

"Not a word. But she knows everything about everyone, my grandmother. And she's good at keeping secrets."

Daphne nodded. In fact, Mrs. Ellis did know everything about everyone at Hembry Castle. And Daphne wouldn't have it any other way.

Edward fed Daphne a spoonful of orange custard. "At least now I have my Christmas story."

"Oh yes?"

"You see, there's this meddlesome ghost that helps his family have a happy Christmas."

"Ghosts and Christmas? Sounds familiar. And predictable."

"Christmas stories are always predictable. But this story hasn't been told before. Not precisely in this way, at least. I think the idea is good enough that it will help me find a new publisher. It might take time, but I will. I can feel it."

"Of course you will. Whatever you do, you'll do it brilliantly, Edward. I've never doubted that for a minute."

And there, in front of everyone, with all manner of propriety cast aside, Edward Ellis kissed Lady Daphne Meriwether on her lips to great applause, even from the Countess.

MRS. ELLIS WATCHED her grandson and her future granddaughter-in-law with great pride, filled to the brim with the young couple's happiness. Her husband handed her a glass of holiday brandy.

"They remind me of us when we were engaged," Augustus Ellis said. "I couldn't keep my eyes from you then, and I cannot keep my eyes from you now."

"Gussie, stop. You'll make me blush." Mrs. Ellis was already ruddy cheeked, more from the brandy than the compliment.

"But you never told Edward." Mr. Ellis didn't sound severe, just surprised. "You said you would tell him so he could tell his lordship and Lady Daphne everything at once."

"I know I did. But Neddie finally told Lady Daphne about George and I decided that perhaps it's best if we deal with one thing at a time."

"You don't really think either Lady Daphne or his lordship will care, do you? Haven't they already proven what large spirits they have?"

"Spirits? Whatever do you mean about spirits?"

"Nothing at all. I simply meant that Lord Staton and Lady Daphne have already shown that they have open hearts and aren't worried so much by appearances as others might be. They accepted Edward as he is, as they'll accept you."

"Of course, you're right, my dear." Mrs. Ellis glanced at the table with the bottles. "I could use another brandy. It's Christmas, you know."

Mr. Ellis laughed as he fetched his wife another drink.

THE GHOST WATCHED his family through the window, the best place for a ghost, after all. The snow had stopped and all around was ice and white, silent but for the wind brushing the trees and seeping through the windowpanes. The ghost exhaled, a sigh of relief. His brother had found pleasant company in Mrs. Gibson. He had begun to make sense of his place as master of Hembry Castle. His niece had her future husband by her side. All was well. He jumped as the creaking door flew open.

"So?" he heard.

"So."

"How do you think you did, Ghost of Hembry Castle? Not so bad for your first time meddling in other people's affairs?"

The ghost nodded toward the window. "Look at them, Mrs. Ellis. Look how happy Edward and Daphne are. Look at how they gaze into each other's eyes. And look at Frederick and Mrs. Gibson." The ghost smiled. "Oh yes, Mrs. Ellis. I think I did very well. Who knows what I might accomplish the next time I meddle? Not bad for someone as selfish as me. Not bad for a ghost."

"You're not selfish," Mrs. Ellis said. "Not at all."

"I'm not a ghost either, come to think of it." He nodded toward Edward and Daphne, who were near the refreshment table whispering in each other's ears. "Do you think they've figured it out yet?"

"They're both sharp-witted. I'd say they know."

"They haven't said anything to Freddie?"

"No. And they aren't going to. His lordship must never know."

He turned to take his leave with one last, wistful glance at his family inside.

"I do so wish I could celebrate with them."

"I know you do, but it's time for you to move on. You're a good man, Richard Meriwether. You've done a good thing. Never forget that, wherever life takes you from here."

He nodded, grateful to Mrs. Ellis. After one more backwards glance, he left the way he came, through the shadows. Then he laughed aloud. Christmas at Hembry Castle was a success after all.

AUTHOR'S NOTES

I had great fun putting my own spin on *A Christmas Carol*. In fact, Edward Ellis is based on a young Charles Dickens, whose grandparents were in service and whose father was always in debt.

Thank you as always to my wonderful readers from all over the world. You are more appreciated than you will ever know.

Some of the books that were helpful to me when I wrote *Christmas at Hembry Castle* were *Dickens* by Peter Ackroyd; *What Jane Austen Ate and Charles Dickens Knew* by Daniel Pool; *How To Be a Victorian: A Dusk-to-Dawn Guide to Victorian Life* by Ruth Goodman; *The Victorian City: Everyday Life in Dickens' London* and *Inside the Victorian Home: A Portrait of Domestic Life in Victorian England* by Judith Flanders; *The Victorian Christmas* by Anna Selby; and *Mrs. Beeton's Cookery Book and Household Guide* by Isabella Beeton.

ABOUT THE AUTHOR

Meredith Allard is the author of the bestselling paranormal historical Loving Husband Trilogy. Her sweet Victorian romance, When It Rained at Hembry Castle, was named a best historical novel by IndieReader. Her first nonfiction book, Painting the Past: A Guide for Writing Historical Fiction, was named a #1 New Release in Authorship and Creativity Self-Help by Amazon. When she isn't writing she's teaching writing, and she has taught writing to students ages five to 75. She loves books, cats, and coffee, though not always in that order. She lives in Las Vegas, Nevada. Visit Meredith online at www.meredithallard.com.